RESCUED BY THE WATER DRAGON PRINCE

ARIA WINTER

JADE WALTZ

Purple Fall
Publishing

Published in the United States by Purple Fall Publishing. Purple Fall Publishing and the Purple Fall Publishing Logos are trademarks and/or registered trademarks of Purple Fall Publishing LLC.-purplefallpublishing.com

Publisher's Cataloging-in-Publication data

Names: Winter, Aria, author. | Waltz, Jade, author.

Title: Rescued By The Water Dragon Prince / Aria Winter & Jade Waltz.

Series: Elemental Dragon Warriors

Description: Purple Fall Publishing, 2021.

Identifiers: ISBN:

978-1-64253-273-9 (pbk.)

978-1-64253-251-7 (ebook)

978-1-64253-499-3 (audiobook)

Subjects: LCSH Space exploration--Fiction. | Human-alien encounters--Fiction. | Dragons--Fiction. | Shapeshifting--Fiction. | Science fiction. | Romance fiction. | BISAC FICTION / Science Fiction / Alien Contact | FICTION / Romance / Science Fiction | FICTION / Romance / Paranormal / Shifters

Classification: LCC PS3623 .I6675 R47 2021 | DDC 813.6--dc23

Cover Design by Kim Cunningham of Atlantis Book Design
PRINTED IN THE UNITED STATES OF AMERICA

Dedication

To my husband: Thank you for all your love and support. You are not just my husband, you are my best friend and my rock. I love you more than anything.

-Aria Winter

To My Husband,
Thank you for being my support and rock during this writing journey. I love you!

-Jade Waltz

CHAPTER 1

TALIA

A soft moan in the darkness draws my attention to the bushes behind us. "Not here," Lilliana whispers breathlessly. "We have company."

I turn my gaze back to the courtyard fire pit, trying to pretend I don't hear the small gasp my friend emits next as her husband—*mate*, I mean—ignores her and continues to do… whatever married couples do during the honeymoon phase of their relationship.

Anna's gaze darts in the direction of the noise and she rolls her green eyes in mock frustration. In reality, I know she feels just like I do. We're both a bit envious of the slice of happiness Lilly seems to have found here with her dragon shifter mate, Varus.

It would be so nice to have someone to come home to—besides my brother, of course. I love him, but I want a mate of my own. I'm twenty-three and I've only been on a handful of dates, each equally disappointing. All the single men on the ship seemed to be more interested in getting me into bed instead of getting to know who I am.

They were always commenting on how beautiful they thought the combination of my chestnut hair and blue eyes were. But none of the ones I dated were interested in marriage or starting a family. And I wasn't just searching for a temporary connection to someone. When I finally give my heart away, I want to know that it's forever. Perhaps that's naïve of me, but I can't help it. It's how I feel.

The Drakarians are different from human men, however. They desire a mate and a family above all else. And when they mate, they mate for life. Lilly is lucky to have found a guy as sweet as Varus. He adores her, dotes on her, and sees to her every need. When he looks at her, his eyes are full of love and devotion like the kind that only exists in myths and legends. I should know—I love art. Particularly the ancient paintings of knights in shining armor staring lovingly at the princess or lady they've pledged themselves to.

Varus is the prince of the Fire Clan, so that makes Lilly the princess. What girl wouldn't love that title? And when it comes with a man who practically worships you, even better.

But that has also become a problem as well. Ever since Varus's Clan rescued us from the desert where we crashed and welcomed us to their kingdom, word has spread far and wide about us humans. Especially the fact that there are eighteen unmated women among us.

Varus found Lilly while she was searching the desert for a place to build a permanent shelter and grow our emergency seeds. Instantly, he recognized her as his fated mate. A glowing fate mark pattern began to swirl on his chest between his two hearts. Apparently, that's how Drakarians recognize their fated mates—or *linaya*, as they call them.

They don't even question the mark's appearance on their

chest because they consider any *linaya* a blessing from the gods.

We're the only species they've found to be biologically compatible with their race, making humans even more valuable to them. According to Varus, a plague swept through their world a few years ago and killed many of their women, leaving most of the survivors barren.

The Drakarian men are handsome, but I find it strange that we're compatible with their species. They are taller than humans, covered in shiny interlocking scales of various colors depending upon their Clan and they have claws instead of nails, a long, tapered tail, dangerous looking fangs and tall horns that spiral up from their heads. Their vertically slit pupils struck me as a bit unnerving at first, but now I'm used to them.

They can also shift into their *draka* form, and when they do they are like every fairy tale dragon I've ever seen in ancient Earth paintings made manifest before me. They are at least five times their normal size in this form.

Because Lilliana is Varus's fated one and we've been found to be biologically compatible, all the unmated Drakarian warriors now eye us with great interest. They seem to be very nice guys from what I can tell, but unfortunately, none have responded to me with that swirling fated mate pattern on their scales.

So, despite their interest, I'm not sure I want to date any of them. If I fall in love with one even though I am not his fated mate, what happens if he finds his fated mate later? I don't want to marry the first warrior who asks me to bond with him—and I've already received many offers. I want to get to know the man I'll choose and make sure we're a good match.

But it's more than just that. The fated mate mark complicates things. Without it, there are no reassurances that bonding to one of these warriors would be permanent.

Besides, Drakarians don't seem to understand the human concept of dating. They do not date. They declare their intentions toward a potential mate and then are either accepted or rejected. Simple as that. They are also extremely possessive when it comes to their mates, or the person they are interested in.

That's why I'm so worried about my friend Skye. She was taken by one of their warriors—Raidyn, prince of the Wind Clan. The Fire Clan sent an ambassador to retrieve her, but the Wind Clan refused to let him speak to her or even see her.

Varus grew up with Raidyn, but they're enemies now. Though Varus has reassured us several times that the Wind Clan prince would never hurt Skye, I can't help but worry about her safety.

I can only hope that members of other Earth and Water Clans are as welcoming as the Fire Clan. Prince Varus and his people have already provided us with homes here, apartments much bigger than the cabins we were assigned on the colony ships.

Despite their hospitality, my younger brother Milo doesn't entirely trust the Drakarians. He thinks they're only helping us because Lilly and Varus have mated.

Lilly is Varus's *linaya*, the first fated mate to be found outside of their race. Varus said many Drakarians from the other Clans are desperate to see us, hoping they will find their *linaya* among us human women.

My brother may be right, but considering how clearly Varus adores my friend, I wonder if it would be so bad to mate a Drakarian warrior myself. Part of me insists that I should stay independent, but another part is hesitant to pass up the opportunity. I just worry that getting tangled up with an alien will only set me up for heartbreak.

So, I've resolved to do my best to settle here and start a new life. And if one of the Drakarian men gets one of those glowing fate marks on his chest for me, I certainly won't fight the bond.

I know the Fire Clan doesn't expect much of us. They provide everything we need: food, water, shelter, clothing. Never once have they asked for anything in return.

However, I've never been one to remain idle.

I'm an engineer and I love my job. I was born with an analytical mind; crunching numbers and solving problems is satisfying work. I've started working with some of the engineers here. I thought they wouldn't respect me since human technology is inferior to theirs, but instead, they've kindly given me modules to study so I can become more familiar with their tech. I've become a part of a collaborative team working to make this city more human-friendly. This city was built for a species that has wings, so we're working together to make lifts, bridges and such to help us humans get around more easily.

Varus and Lilly take their seats on the bench beside me. Her lips are swollen from kissing her mate, and it doesn't escape me that her long, ginger hair is slightly disheveled. She turns to her mate and the red scales of his cheeks darken a shade as he smiles down at her. When I first saw him, his onyx horns struck me as sinister, but now I find that I barely notice the differences between his people and mine.

Lilly smiles at Anna and me. "Why don't you two spend the night here in the castle?"

It's tempting, especially since I love spending time in the palace gardens. They are like an oasis in the middle of the desert. The entire courtyard is covered in green and purple trees, bushes, and flowering plants, a lovely contrast to the deep-red and orange walls of the palace.

I mull over her question, twirling a glowing blue flower I picked from the garden in my hand. The rich color reminds me of Prince Llyr of the Water Clan. He's staying here at the castle with his sister, Noralla, and I've had the pleasure of speaking to him on several occasions. I'd love to stay the night and spend more time with him, but I need to return to my apartment and my brother, Milo. We have both had trouble sleeping lately, each of us still dealing with the loss of our parents when our ship was attacked. I don't want to leave Milo alone with his grief. He's the only family I have left.

I face Varus and Lilly. "Thanks for the offer, but I need to get back to Milo."

"Thanks," Anna adds, "but I think I'm going to the med clinic and then back to my apartment. Ranas is supposed to give me a med scanner so I can get more familiar with the settings."

Anna's like me. We're both dedicated to learning how to incorporate Drakarian tech and methods into our professions. She was our ship's doctor and now she's studying under Healer Ranas to practice medicine here.

Varus nods in acknowledgment then returns his attention to Lilly.

I sigh. It's so romantic how he regards her like she is everything to him. I wonder how it feels to be so treasured.

I stand and embrace Lilly warmly. "I'll see you tomorrow."

Anna hugs her too, and then starts off for the med center to meet Ranas.

Varus dips his chin in a subtle bow, his gaze quickly drifting back to his mate.

With another wistful sigh, I head back into the castle

from the gardens. I turn the corner toward the exit and nearly collide with Llyr.

Piercing silver eyes meet mine, and I bite back a sigh. I could get lost in his gaze forever. His vertically slit pupils contract and then expand as he looks down at me. "Forgive my carelessness." He bows slightly, like a gentleman. "I did not realize you were here."

My cheeks heat in embarrassment as his intense gaze holds mine. I open my mouth to speak, but the words die in my throat. Llyr is incredibly handsome. He's taller than any human man I've ever met; the aquamarine horns that spiral up from his head only add to his height, accentuating his fine brow, nose, and cheeks. His deep blue hair hangs down to his broad shoulders. His entire body is lean yet muscular. A long white robe covers most of his scales. Their dappled blue color reminds me of the tropical oceans back on Earth.

Nervously, I tuck a stray tendril of my long, brown hair behind my ear.

I'm surprised that Llyr is dressed. Drakarians think nothing of nudity. Lilly told me they change back and forth between their humanoid and *draka* forms so often that wearing clothes is not convenient. Their *draka* form is at least five times larger than a man, so clothing would only shred when they shift.

As I study Llyr, I can't deny that I find the lethal edge to his handsome features attractive. Black claws tip the five toes and fingers on his hands and feet. When his lips part in a smile, I can't help but notice the sharp row of fangs that line his mouth. Nonetheless, he is nothing short of devastatingly gorgeous.

Completely mesmerized by his smile, it takes me a moment to realize that I'm openly gaping at him. I blink several times to regain my senses and then stumble over my

7

words. "No. Uh. I'm sorry. I—*I'm* the one who nearly ran into you."

He tips his head to the side. "Where were you off to in such a hurry?"

"I, uh—it's getting late, so I was heading home." Funny how I only moved in days ago, but I already consider my apartment home.

"It is dark. Would you like me to accompany you?"

His question catches me off guard. Is there a reason I would need an escort at night? Are there desert predators that might creep into the city after dark and try to eat me? "I thought it was safe here in the capital."

He frowns. "It is, but I have heard that your kind see poorly in low-lighting conditions."

I struggle to suppress a huff of frustration. While that's technically true—humans don't see as well in the dark as Drakarians—I hate being reminded of how inferior a race they consider us. I can't count how many times a Drakarian has commented on my lack of scales, wings, claws, or fangs. I've even had a few ask me how my people have managed to survive as a species with our lack of natural defenses.

But rather than be offended, I offer Llyr a friendly smile. He's only trying to be nice. "Thanks, but you don't have to. I should be just fine on my own." Drakarian women are fierce, I've heard. I certainly don't want Llyr to think I'm afraid of walking home in the dark.

"I insist," he says. "Besides, I believe I would enjoy a walk. Unless"—he arches a brow—"you would prefer to fly."

To be honest, I would indeed prefer to fly, but I'm too shy to tell him that. He's handsome, the most attractive man I've ever met, but as my gaze drops to his chest, I note that no swirling fate bond pattern glows on his scales. So he's not the one for me, and I would rather keep things friendly between us. Flying seems like an intimate step because I'd have to trust him enough not to drop me.

I've spoken with Llyr many times. If I let myself, I know it would be so easy to fall in love with him. But I can't give him my heart while I know he could end up fated to someone else. So, I've convinced myself to keep some distance from him.

Besides, I enjoy walking at night. Without the scorching sun overhead, the temperature is pleasant. Also, I don't like the idea of relying on Drakarians to get around the city. They're friendly people, but eventually, they might grow tired of helping us humans. That's why I'm working with some of their engineers to make life in the capital a bit easier for my crew. This place is beautiful, but it wasn't built for a race without wings.

"I think I'd prefer to walk."

An emotion flashes behind Llyr's eyes, but it's gone too quickly for me to know what it was. He dips his chin in agreement. "Then we shall walk. If you do not mind the company, that is," he adds with a grin.

My heart flutters. Of course, I don't mind. I enjoy talking with Llyr and I want to spend as much time with him as I can before he leaves Fire Clan territory. My gaze darts briefly again to his chest, hoping to see the swirling fate mark, but I find nothing. And I probably never will. Despite the desperate ache in my heart, I somehow manage to reply, "I'd love to walk with you."

CHAPTER 2

TALIA

When I first learned of the fate bond, I was convinced Llyr would be the one for me. We instantly clicked when I met him. And he checks off every box for me: intelligent, thoughtful, tall, handsome, *blue*. I added that last requirement after meeting him.

He's a prince, just like Varus, but that's where the similarities end. Varus is charismatic: the kind of person who attracts people to his circle with his disarming smile. Llyr, on the other hand, is pensive almost to the point of brooding. He has a quiet, intense thoughtfulness that draws me in.

He's supposed to return to his Water Clan territory soon, and I'm already dreading his departure. Once he leaves, I don't know when or if I'll ever see him again. Lilly said that according to Varus, it's rare for Drakarians of different Clans to visit each other's territories. Llyr only traveled here because his sister was betrothed to Varus before he discovered Lilly. Now that they've formalized an alliance between their Clans, he has no reason to stay any longer.

"I'll bet you're looking forward to going home," I tell him. Though I phrase it as a statement, my tone holds a question as well. Deep down, I wonder if he'll miss me as much as I'll miss him.

His gaze sweeps toward the desert. "I do miss the deep oceans of our Clan's territory. It is strange to be in a place with so little water. Even the wind here is devoid of moisture."

He's right. The desert air that drifts up from the valley is cool and dry against my skin. I close my eyes briefly, imagining the dull roar of the sea. My favorite places to explore in the virtual reality rooms on the ship were the tropical waters of Earth before it was poisoned beyond saving.

Llyr said his castle sits on the edge of a cliff that borders the ocean below. Whereas the palace district here is elevated above the rest of the city. Various buildings and houses, shaped from earthen brown and red clay, stand proudly atop the mesa. The style is simple yet elegant in its design and similar in style to Varus's castle.

I wonder if the architecture of Llyr's home is anything like this. I've always been an explorer at heart, imagining all the new places we would discover once we found a permanent home. I'd love to see where he lives, and I wonder if his city is divided like it seems to be here.

The wealthier citizens make their home near Varus's castle, whereas the remainder of the Fire Clan lives in the valley below, along the river that curves around the base. Verdant fields of rich farmlands, fed from the water's canals, dot the landscape. Across the river lies a steep plateau. The deep orange and crimson layers of rock are beautiful to behold during the day. I should know; I scan the landscape often from my bedroom, trying to decide the best location for constructing a bridge that spans the river.

We walk in silence, and while it's not uncomfortable, I feel the need to start a conversation anyway, especially since my time with him is limited. I open my mouth to speak, but Llyr beats me to it.

He turns to me. "I've heard you are working with the Fire Clan engineers to create lifts to allow your people to be able to move up and down the mesa and access the different levels of the city. That is an excellent idea. You are brilliant, Talia."

I smile brightly, thrilled at the compliment. "If we're going to live here, we can't rely on you guys to do all the heavy lifting for us humans."

His brow furrows softly. "But your people are not heavy. I've heard it is no burden to carry you upon our backs."

I grin, amused at his literal interpretation of my sentence. "It's an idiom," I explain. "It just means that we need to be able to get around without relying on Drakarians to help us. Even if you don't see us as a burden, we certainly don't want to become one. And if this is to be our home, we need to be able to travel independently."

He stops abruptly and his silver eyes meet mine. "Your people are not a burden to us. We would never consider you as such. Ever," he states firmly. "If anything, you are a blessing."

My expression falls as I realize he's talking about the possibility of humans breeding with Drakarians.

While most of the women in my crew find the dragon-men handsome, several have voiced concerns that they might only be interested in our wombs.

Deep down, I want to believe that it isn't true, that they are good people who want to help us, and our compatibility is just a bonus. But I can't entirely ignore the fact of their belief that we're the answer to preventing their species' extinction. By studying my crew, their Healers have determined that we're not only capable of having interspecies children, but that Drakarian genes would be dominant for up to seven generations.

Llyr leans closer to regard me. "I have upset you."

I've never been one to hold back my thoughts, so I decide I won't start now. I meet his blue eyes evenly. "My friend Skye was taken by a Drakarian. And Varus thinks it's because of the fate bond."

"Yes. I suspect this as well."

"However, I'm worried that he may have taken her just because she's female, and he found out we're compatible with your species."

He takes my hand and I'm surprised by the silken texture of his scales against my skin. He's standing so close to me now that the warmth of his body radiates into mine as he stares at me with a pained expression. "I am sorry your friend was taken, Talia. But I promise you that no Drakarian would ever force a female to become his mate. It is simply not done. Even before the plague, females were worshipped and treasured among our people."

"Then why do you think he took her? Why hasn't he brought her back?"

"Prince Raidyn is a good male. He would not have taken her unless he had good reason."

His words shock me. "So it's all right to take someone against their will if you have a *good reason*"—I emphasize the last two words with air quotations—"like a fate bond?" I can't hide the anger in my tone.

His eyes fly wide, aghast. "No. I meant that we suspect something happened between her and the human male, John." He practically spits out John's name as if even the sound disgusts him. "If Raidyn recognized Skye as his fated one, that would have triggered his protective instincts. He would only have taken her if he believed she was in danger."

The rest of the crew and I have questioned John's story, especially after he was reluctant to give Varus details about how Skye was taken. John was the only witness. Varus has insinuated that John was trying to harm her in some way, and the fact that John hesitated in his answer was a big red flag for me.

"Yeah, John's story doesn't quite add up," I admit before I realize I've spoken aloud.

Llyr studies me in concern. "You believe John may be dangerous?"

"I—I don't—" I start to say *I don't think so,* but the truth is, he's been acting aggressively lately, especially since we all came to the city. He keeps trying to convince us that we need to leave, that we're better off on our own. I think he feels threatened by these Drakarians. After all, before they showed up, John was one of only a handful of men who survived the crash. Clearly, he liked those odds, since we were starting a new life here on this planet. He probably thought he was Adam surrounded by several Eves, so to speak, ready to grow our small population.

"I'm not sure," I finally reply.

"Would you like him removed from the human quarters?" Llyr asks.

The human quarters. That's what this part of the city has been called since we moved into the apartments. I know the Fire Clan is eager to integrate us into their society, but sometimes I feel a bit like an exotic animal in a nature reserve.

"Not yet," I tell him. "I'm hoping we will find out what happened when Skye returns. Hear her side of the story, you know."

Llyr doesn't comment, but he doesn't have to. The look in his eyes tells me that he disagrees. Like Varus, he thinks John is a threat. Although I'm reluctant to admit it, I have a strong feeling John would be glad if Skye never came back at all.

"If you change your mind, we will make certain he is removed immediately," Llyr says. "I dislike the idea of you feeling unsafe in any way."

I'm not sure how to respond to that, so I offer a generic "Thanks." Still, his concern touches me; he's acting almost like a protective boyfriend. The thought makes my insides flutter and my heart quickens its pace as I stare up at him.

"What does this"—he mimics my air quotations—"mean?"

I laugh at his quizzical expression. "It emphasizes important words in conversation."

"Oh," he replies thoughtfully. His expression turns solemn and he leans down slightly as he raises his hands, crooking the first two fingers to make air quotations. "I vow to protect you from danger, Talia."

I would laugh if my stomach weren't full of butterflies. If my heart was beating quickly before, it's practically racing now. My entire body heats as I beam. "Thank you, Llyr."

He dips his head in a regal bow. "I will do anything to make certain you are safe," he makes air quotations again. "My vow."

My heart feels like it plummets and soars all at once. I wish desperately that Llyr could be mine. I drop my gaze to his chest, praying once again for the swirling glow of the fate mark pattern to appear, but it doesn't. I bite back a sigh of frustration, remembering how soon he'll be leaving.

If he were human, things would be simple. We could just continue to get to know one another, start dating, and then... My heart clenches. I'm falling for this man—I can't help it. I want to know everything about him even if he can't be mine.

"Tell me about your home." I force a smile to my face to hide my sadness. "What is it like in the Water Clan territory?"

He turns his gaze toward the desert again. Although I

cannot see the valley in the dark, I've stared across the crimson ocean of sand several times. There's no denying that the harsh landscape holds a certain beauty, but it's also terribly bleak.

I'm curious about what the other Clans' lands are like. More importantly, I want to hear about Llyr's home so I can imagine him there once he's gone.

"My home sits atop a cliff that overlooks the sea below. At night, the cool breeze carries in the saline scent of the ocean and the sound of the waves crashing against the rocks along the shoreline. The waters are a crystal-clear, deep shade of blue. Like your eyes." A smile quirks his lips. "It is beautiful. But then again, I suppose every Clan thinks their lands beautiful. There is a kind of beauty to be found here in the desert as well," he adds thoughtfully. "Do you not agree?"

I shrug. "It is pretty here, but I'd love to see the ocean someday."

He flashes his devastatingly handsome smile. "I could take you... if you wish."

I open my mouth to reply when the door to my apartment opens abruptly, startling me.

"I was worried about you," Milo says. He blinks in surprise then levels a dark glare at Llyr. "What's he doing here?"

Milo doesn't completely trust the Drakarians because one of them took Skye. I guess I can't blame him; she was his friend, too. He made me promise not to get involved with one until we're sure they are what they claim to be—good people.

"Milo," I snap, incensed by his terrible manners. "Llyr was just walking me home."

My brother narrows his blue eyes as his gaze rakes over Llyr's form. "Well, thanks. I guess that was... nice of you," he reluctantly admits. He wraps a hand around my forearm, pulling me inside. "Now, goodnight."

I can't help but notice Llyr's stunned expression at Milo's abrupt and rude dismissal. So I quickly offer, "Goodnight, and thank you, Llyr."

He dips his chin just before Milo practically slams the door in his face.

CHAPTER 3

LLYR

Devastation washes through me as the door slams shut, leaving me alone on the walkway. My female, the one who has captured my hearts, already has a mate. I look down at my chest. I wondered why I did not glow with the fated mark the moment I first laid eyes upon her, but now I understand. She is already claimed.

She can never be mine.

With each step back to the castle, the terrible ache in my chest grows even stronger. I wanted to walk her home so that I might ask if I may court her in the ways of her people. But now that I know she has a mate, I've never known such despair.

When I return to the castle, I find my sister, Noralla, along with Varus and his fated mate—his linaya—Lilliana.

Noralla's blue hair, which is normally long and free like mine is now in a series of intricate braids that are swept up and twisted around her head, accentuating her horns.

Lilliana—Varus's mate—usually has her hair in this style, and a grin tilts my lips to think that she must be the one who did this to my sister's hair. It is nice to see that she and Noralla get along so well.

As I enter the room, my gaze drops to Varus's chest. The fated mate pattern glows brightly on his scales, directly between his two hearts. His human mate regards him lovingly.

Subconsciously, I rub my open palm over my chest as if I can somehow ease the hollow ache that now plagues me. When Talia arrived at the castle on the back of one of Varus's warriors, freshly rescued from their crash site in the desert, I was so sure she was mine. I felt our connection deep in my soul the moment I saw her. With her long, silken brown hair, skin the color of light sand, and eyes as blue as the sea, I have never seen a more beautiful female than Talia.

Closing my eyes, I remember the first time we spoke. She gave me a dazzling smile that rivaled the brightness of the sun. Each time we have talked since then, my feelings for her have only deepened. I have found it difficult not to confess them to her. Talia is brilliant, beautiful and kind. She is a beautiful light in a world that has experienced so much darkness.

I lost many friends and family to the Great Plague that swept across our planet a few cycles ago. Since then, it has been difficult to find joy in each day, knowing that so many are gone.

Talia's people have lost much as well after their colony ships were attacked by pirates. And yet, despite their terrible losses, she still manages to greet each day with a smile and an attitude of perseverance. I admire and am in awe of this innate strength in her. She may be physically smaller than a Drakarian female, but that does not mean she is not strong in other ways.

My hearts recognized her as mine the first time I saw her. Immediately, I looked for the fated mark on my chest, but it did not appear. I've heard it does not always happen instantly, so I held on to the hope that it would come. However, I know now that it never will. Even though my soul knows she belongs at my side, we can never be together. Another has already claimed her.

I study my twin sister, Noralla. At least I will not have to part with her. She was supposed to enter into a betrothal with Prince Varus to ally our two Clans through bonding, but now that he is mated to Lilliana, I cannot deny that I am glad. Noralla can return with me to our home. I could hardly stand the thought of leaving my sister—my best friend and confidante—alone in the land of the red desert sands.

We are of the Water Clan; the desert does not suit our kind.

As if sensing my troubled thoughts, she turns to me. "Is something wrong?"

Varus and Lilliana look at me as well.

My hearts are so heavy that my first inclination is to tell them everything is wrong. Nothing will ever be right again. Not when I have found my fated one only to discover that she cannot be mine.

"No." The lie burns like acid on my tongue. Normally, I share everything with my sister, but not this. I am too aggrieved to voice my sorrow.

I consider consulting Varus but realize he would not understand. He is happily mated; fortunately, his linaya was not tethered to another when he found her. While I am glad for him, I cannot help but feel jealous, as well. Why would the gods do this to me? Why fate me to one who already belongs to someone else?

Perhaps it is a test from the gods. If so, I am close to failing. I considered this when I left her apartment. On my way back to the castle, I thought of several different ways I could lure her away from her mate and convince her to be mine.

Deep down, I know that any honorable male would accept what fate has dealt him and move on. But I cannot. Even knowing that the gods would never condone the stealing of another's mate, deep in my heart I desire more than anything for her to be mine. Noralla and I will be leaving soon to return to our Clan, and I am loath to leave Talia behind.

Despite that she is already mated, I long to spend as much time as I can in her presence. The pull of the bond is strong. Soon, I will be forced to leave her, and then I will need to learn how to breathe again. How does one go on living when one's linaya is mated to another male? Even now, the thought is almost more than I can bear.

Varus kisses his human mate and I lower my gaze. It is difficult to witness the happiness before me that I know will never be mine. My mood is somber and I wish only to be alone with my despair. I glance at Varus and my sister. "I bid you goodnight."

"Llyr?" Noralla calls after me as I start down the hallway. "Are you certain everything is all right?"

"Yes," I lie again, desperate to lock myself in my room and wallow in my thoughts. "I will see you in the morning, dear sister."

"Goodnight."

When I wake in the morning, I feel as if I never slept. I tossed and turned fitfully all night, dreaming of Talia. Noralla and I leave soon, and I wish there is some way to convince her to come with me. I do not care that she has a mate. I should, but

I cannot be honorable and simply leave her alone. Not when my feelings for her are so strong.

I'm desperate to keep Talia nearby. I refuse to leave without knowing if I will ever see her again. As I sit around the table with Varus, Lilliana, and my sister, a plan formulates in my mind.

I turn to Varus. "Do you remember when our Clans used to gather each cycle for a celebration of peace?"

Varus nods. How could he forget? We used to rotate which territory would host the gathering, and it was last held here in the capital of the Fire Clan. After the last celebration, Prince Raidyn and his mother were caught in a sandstorm returning to their lands. His mother died as a result and Raidyn's face was permanently scarred. He still blames Varus's Clan, which is why they are no longer friends.

His green gaze holds mine as he patiently waits for me to continue.

"I thought that perhaps we might hold these festivities again." Remembering the female who was stolen by Prince Raidyn of the Wind Clan, I quickly add, "Excluding the Wind Clan, of course. At least until we find out exactly what happened to the human female whom Raidyn took."

Varus leans closer. "Prince Raidyn and I have had our differences in the past, but I know this for a fact: he would never harm a female."

While I agree that Raidyn would never do such a thing, I am surprised at how vehemently Varus defends his former friend. They used to be as close as brothers. Perhaps they are not truly enemies now after all.

Varus continues. "Raidyn would only have taken her if she were in danger, and I suspect the human John may be to blame for that." He looks at his mate. "Lilliana also suspects this male is not being entirely truthful about the events surrounding the disappearance of her friend."

Despite my resolution to remain calm, my protective instincts surge as I remember how close Talia lives to the creature named John. I grip the chair's armrests so tightly the wood begins to creak as I give Varus a pointed look. "Then why is this male allowed to live among their people? The females are not safe. He could harm them."

Lilliana frowns. "Until we can talk to Skye, we don't have any proof. You cannot condemn someone based on mere suspicion."

"Why not?" My voice emerges harsher than I intended.

Varus answers with a low warning growl, and I immediately realize my mistake. I bow my head. "Forgive me. I am simply worried about the females."

"The females?" Varus arches a brow. "Or one in particular?"

I turn away from his gaze, feigning ignorance. "Of whom do you speak?"

He leans in, his lips tipping up in a sly smirk. "I've seen the way you eye one of them." He drops his gaze to my chest. "Your mark has not appeared, but I suspect it soon will."

Noralla smiles at me and Lilliana grins as she nods in agreement.

I gape at them. Is it so obvious that I desire Talia? With a heavy sigh, I sit back in my chair. "What you are suggesting can never be."

"Why?" Noralla is the first to ask.

"Because—"

I stop abruptly when one of Varus's guards rushes in. "Prince Raidyn has appeared. He carries a human female upon his back—the one who was taken. Rakan is escorting him here."

Varus shoots up from his chair and immediately pulls his small human mate behind him as if to shield her. "He is not supposed to be here. His father declined our invitation to

24

meet, and they sent our ambassador away when he went to inquire about the female. Why is he here now?"

"I do not know, my prince," the guard answers. "But they are approaching the city."

Varus turns to Lilliana. "Please wait here, my linaya. Where it is safe."

"No," she protests. "I won't let you go alone. If Raidyn is as honorable as you said, he won't hurt me. I need to see my friend. I need to know that Skye is all right."

Varus wraps a protective arm around Lilliana but reluctantly nods. "Fine. But please stay close and do not leave my side."

He lifts his gaze to my sister and me. In his expression, I read the question he does not pose. He is wondering if we would take the side of the Fire Clan in a dispute with the Wind Clan.

"Whatever happens, you have the support of the Water Clan," I reassure him.

He bows his head slightly in acknowledgment then heads for the front courtyard with Lilliana.

Noralla sends me a hesitant glance. "I do not like this. Why has Raidyn come alone?"

I don't like it either. "I do not know. Although Raidyn is not King of the Wind Clan, he has been quietly leading in his father's stead ever since the king went mad after the death of the queen." I pause. "I hope there is no unrest among their people."

A deafening roar splits the air, stopping my hearts.

Noralla's head snaps toward the castle entrance. "What was that?"

Another guard bursts into the room. "The Wind Clan is attacking the human quarter of the city. They're trying to abduct the females."

Alarm bursts through me as an image of Talia being

ripped into the sky by one of Raidyn's brethren overtakes my mind. "Stay here," I yell at Noralla, rushing toward the entrance.

My sister does not argue because she understands. Noralla is fully capable of fighting and defending herself, but if I fall in battle, she is the only remaining heir to our throne and one of only a limited number of females among our people. Her safety cannot be risked.

A third guard ushers Lilliana and a strange human female with golden hair past me into the castle. "Take them to my sister," I order. "She will keep them safe."

He nods and I turn once more toward the city. Fire burns in my veins as I shift and extend my wings to take flight.

I release a bellowing roar of challenge as I ascend into the sky to join the battle. I will defend the human females or die in the attempt. I cannot allow the Wind Clan to steal them away without resistance. I head toward the human quarter of the city, searching for Talia. If anyone dares try to harm or take her, I will rip his throat out with my bare fangs.

Rakan, the captain of Varus's guard, falls into line beside me. "The Wind Clan has come to kidnap the females." His red eyes are frantic as he scans the streets; I know whom he seeks. He is like me—in love with a human, but his fate mark has yet to appear.

Panic coils tightly in my chest as I catch Talia's scent in the air. Rage blisters through me as I watch one of the Wind Clan warriors heading straight for her. Her scream stops my hearts as he scoops her up with his claws, wrapping his talons tightly around her struggling form.

Furiously flapping my wings, I cannot fly fast enough. The distance between us is too great. A swarm of warriors clouds the sky, making it impossible to find a direct path. I dip and weave through the battle, dodging the individual skirmishes as I work my way to her.

Frostfire licks at the back of my throat as rage builds deep in my chest. I will die before I let them take her. I release a thunderous battle cry as I race toward my linaya.

She is mine!

CHAPTER 4

TALIA

A deafening roar splits the air and I rush outside to see what the commotion is. Drakarians in *draka* form, with scales in varying shades of white and gray, descend upon the city. My heart stops when I realize who they are—the *draka* of the Wind Clan. The ones who stole my friend Skye.

My heart pounds with fear as sirens ring in my ears. Screams fill the air as people scatter in every direction, trying to find shelter while fire and destruction rain down from overhead.

Varus's Fire Clan warriors meet the invaders head-on, the sound of their clashing forms like booming thunder as they lock their talons together and tear into flesh with claws and fangs.

Blood falls all around them, painting the naturally red buildings and streets with obsidian-black stains.

My friend Holly rushes toward me with terror filled eyes.

"In here!" I yell, extending my arm to pull her inside the building.

The heavy beat of a draka's wings overhead whips up dust and debris. Sunlight reflects off the iridescent white scales of the Wind Clan warrior as he comes up behind her.

I race toward her, my hand outstretched to grasp hers. "Holly!"

The tips of her fingers brush against mine as the Wind warrior wraps his talons around her form. Her eyes meet mine and I jump toward her, but too late as he rips her from the ground.

A terrified scream erupts from her throat as he spirals up toward the clouds.

One of the Fire warriors breaks away from his opponent to go after her. The orange-red coloring of his scales and deep-crimson eyes tell me that it is Rakan, Varus's lead guard —the man that has been falling all over himself to please Holly ever since we arrived. "Release her!" he roars as he gives chase. "If you hurt her, I will end you!"

Another Wind dragon flies low, releasing a torrent of fire in his wake. The ground explodes beneath the assault, showering brick and debris. "Everyone inside," I yell. "We have to take shelter."

The apartments are small enough that we may be able to hide out from the Wind Clan if they remain in their *draka* form. They're too large to fit through the doors, so we might have a chance.

Two other women race toward us. My brother rushes to meet them halfway, wielding a long piece of pipe. I don't know where he got it or how much use that will be against a dragon, but I also understand that he's desperate to save them. "Aria. Maya. Hurry!" he urges, ushering them toward our apartment.

Maya has almost reached him when two Wind and Fire

dragons crash into the building beside her. The entire structure crumbles inward, raining down lethal chunks of rock. She trips and sprawls forward on the pavement.

"Get up. Hurry," Milo calls.

She struggles to stand but collapses as she reaches for her ankle, rubbing the joint as if in pain. "Help me!"

Milo rushes toward her. He's nearly there when a Wind dragon comes up behind her, scooping her into his massive talons. Her terrified eyes lock on to mine and I watch helplessly as he takes her away.

A great rush of wind at my back pushes me forward, and I barely catch myself from falling. I spin toward the source as my brother's voice rings out, "Talia, no!"

My eyes widen as a Wind dragon wraps his deadly talons around my form and lifts me off the ground. The wind whips through my hair as he beats his powerful wings and ascends into the sky, high above the city. Milo frantically waves his arms below, shouting curses into the air and demanding the dragon let me go.

No matter what the Wind Clan has planned for me, I won't go easily. I punch and bite at my captor's hand, but it's no use. His scales are impenetrable, and in this form, he's at least six times my size. I'm sure my pitiful attempts to free myself are laughable compared to his strength.

I watch in helpless shock as a blue Water dragon races toward us from across the city. My heart soars. It's Llyr—it must be.

"Llyr!"

"Talia! I'm coming!"

Llyr furiously beats his powerful wings as he rushes to save me. He slams into my captor's side at full speed.

The Wind dragon roars in pain and loosens his grip, sending me spiraling in freefall.

The air whips around me as I drop with dizzying speed

toward the ground. I only have a moment to accept my impending death when I hit something solid. A horrible *crack* pierces the air as I land on another Wind dragon's back. Searing pain rips through my entire body, stealing the breath from my lungs.

Tears sting my eyes and blur my vision as I grit my teeth against the pain. Despite my agony, my resolve is absolute. I will not go quietly, and I will not be a slave. I can easily guess what the Wind Dragons want from us—we're female and breeding-compatible. He banks toward the desert, but I have already accepted what I must do. I will not go. I would rather die than be taken. Despite the unbearable pain in my side, I force myself to sit up.

The wind claws at my form as I push myself up to standing.

"What are you—" the dragon calls over his shoulder, but he's too late.

As soon as I stand, a rush of air pulls me off his back. Suddenly, I'm falling again, tumbling with dizzying speed toward the crimson sand below.

CHAPTER 5

LLYR

I watch Talia struggling to stand on the Wind warrior's back in blank horror. At first, I don't understand, but then she pushes herself up the rest of the way. Raising her arms, she lets go entirely. Time slows as the wind rips her away and she drops in freefall, spiraling toward the desert below.

My hearts stop and then begin pounding as I race toward her. She screams but it's quickly swallowed by the air racing past us. If she hits the ground, she is dead. I know I cannot fail her.

Folding my wings tightly against my back, I dive. The scent of Talia's fear fills my nostrils and panic constricts my chest as we spiral toward the earth. In this moment, I know that I will save her or die trying. My body is large enough to cushion her fall should we slam into the ground. I will sacrifice my life for her; I refuse to let death claim my linaya this day.

Gritting my teeth, I can hear nothing over the pounding

of my own pulse in my ears as time slows and stretches out between each beat of my hearts. I twist my body and swoop beneath her. Snapping my wings open I catch her on my back, abruptly halting our descent.

She lands on my body with a sickening *crack*. A piercing cry full of pain and anguish escapes her. The sound threatens to stop my hearts, for I realize she is badly injured and broken. "You are safe," I call out, offering the only solace that I can in this moment. "Hold tightly to me. I'm taking you to the Healer."

Worry beats at my chest when she doesn't immediately reply.

"Please hurry," she manages in a voice so low I almost miss it.

Her words give speed to my flight as I race back to the castle, inwardly cursing myself for not having rescued her sooner. Not only that, but I caused her further injury by catching her as I did. The memory of her body breaking upon my back makes me shudder to think what injuries she might have sustained.

"We're almost there, Talia," I call over my shoulder as the Med Center comes into view.

Curse Raidyn and all the Wind Clan. How dare they attack us and try to steal the human females? They are sentient beings, not animals. They will pay for mistreating them—my vow.

As soon as I reach the medical center's courtyard, I find several of the Fire Clan warriors already tending to injured human females. The Healers and medics are rushing back and forth between them, assessing the extent of their wounds.

I notice there are several injured Drakarians as well, but it is the humans that worry me most. They are not built as strongly as my people and, from what I understand, they do not heal as quickly either.

Instantly, I shift into my two-legged form. Twisting my body, I catch her by the waist before she even touches the ground. As carefully as I can, I carry Talia toward the others. Her delicate hands cling weakly to my forearm. "Llyr," she mumbles. "Please. It hurts."

Her muted pleas tear at my hearts. I wish that I could take this pain from her. I cannot bear to see her in so much agony. "You are safe, Talia. I have you. I'll find a Healer to mend your injuries."

The med center is located not far from the palace. Normally, it is calm and quiet out here, but today it is not. Holding Talia firmly to my chest, I push through the doors and into absolute chaos. Every bed appears to be full.

Several groans and whimpers of pain fill the air as patients wait to be tended. There are so many that are terribly wounded, I wonder how the Healers and medics will treat them all.

Surely, they will need help. I hope they have already sent for aid from the Earth Clan. They would be the logical choice since so many of their people are natural Healers. They are the only Clan who possess the ability to breathe healing fire, able to mend injuries in this way.

Frantically, I scan the area, desperate to find Healer Ranas. With his deep green scales, he is easy to find since he is one of the few Earth Clan warriors here, surrounded by so many red and orange colored Fire Clan warriors. I race toward him, crying out, "Ranas, hurry! Talia needs you!"

His eyes go wide as they land on Talia, and he races in my direction, meeting me halfway. He pulls at her smaller form, trying to take her from my arms. "Give her to me," he urges.

My hearts clench as she releases an anguished cry when I

attempt to transfer her to him. "She is mine. Please, you must heal her."

Her eyelids flutter open, her gaze unfocused as she holds on to my arm with all the strength she has left, refusing to let go. "Llyr."

"It is all right, Talia. Healer Ranas will help you. You are safe."

Ranas's green eyes dart briefly to my chest, and I know what he is searching for. He's checking whether the fated mark pattern glows across my scales. Although it does not, I know in my hearts that this female is my linaya—my fated one.

"Put her down here." He gestures to the bed.

As gently as possible, I lay her down. Her weight is so slight it worries me. Varus spoke truth when he told me these human females are fragile compared to our species. And yet, there is strength in my linaya, who grits her teeth to stifle another groan of pain.

Fear batters at my mind when Ranas's eyes widen as he runs the scanner over her smaller form, studying her many injuries. He forces his expression into an impassive mask and then murmurs to her, "You are safe here. I will heal you."

He lifts a worried gaze to me. "She has several fractures on her ribs, puncture wounds, cuts, and abrasions across her body."

Emotions lodge in my throat, but I somehow manage to speak around them. "Will she be all right?"

He nods. "Yes. But I must call upon more of my brethren from the Earth Clan to help us tend all the injured. I do not have the energy to treat them all by myself."

She winces slightly as he pulls back her robe.

I struggle to suppress a low growl. I know he is only trying to tend her injuries, but it is difficult to contain the protective and possessive instincts I feel toward her.

Only Drakarians of the Earth Clan possess healing fire. They have always remained neutral when war has broken out between the rest of the Clans because they do not wield the power of destruction as we do. Though they breathe fire, they are nowhere near as powerful as the rest of us who breathe either flame or frostfire.

They possess the ability to heal and mend, not ruin and injure. But even their healing strength has a limit. An Earth Drakarian's energy wanes with each use of the healing fire. I understand why Ranas requires more help from his people— there are many injured human females and Drakarians gathered here.

Varus's female had been attacked by a sand tarkin when he rescued her. He told me that humans cannot heal as quickly as we do, even with the aid of Earth Clan Healers. Curling my hands into fists at my side, I curse the Wind Clan again.

As my gaze travels over Talia's bare torso, panic quickens my heart rate. Her normally pale skin is heavily bruised in many places. I clench my jaw as I notice five shallow puncture wounds from the Wind warrior's talons. Unable to stop myself, I reach out and touch her cheek, brushing my fingers lightly over the many scratch marks that mar her beautiful face.

She leans into my touch as Ranas blows his healing fire across her injuries. The blue-green flame's effect is a welcome sight. Already, the deep crease in her brow begins to smooth as he takes her pain away.

When he is finished, he addresses her. "The healing fire may make you sleepy. If it does, I suggest you allow yourself to rest so you may heal faster."

"I will," she replies. "Thank you."

As Ranas leaves to tend another patient, Talia's mate rushes into the medical center. His wild eyes scan the room

ARIA WINTER & JADE WALTZ

and as soon as they land upon her, he races toward the bed. He hugs her tightly, and I growl low in warning when she winces in pain. "Are you all right?" he asks.

"I will be," she mumbles against him, "if you let go of me."

I growl again at this male's incompetence. He is careless and does not deserve her. Can he not see that she is injured?

"Oh. Sorry," he mumbles, seeming scattered. "I was just... Thank the Stars you're all right." He spins to face me, his expression suddenly thunderous. "Screw you, dragon-man. This is all your fault."

"I—" I open my mouth to protest, but what can I say? He is right. It is my fault she is so grievously injured. If I had reached her sooner, she probably would not have been hurt so badly.

He advances on me. "Ever since we got here, your men have done nothing but eye our women like they're pieces of meat. And now, one of your Clans tried to kidnap them. How dare you? I knew your warm welcome was too good to be true! All this hospitality was meant to cover up your sick plan to use the women as breeding stock now that you know we're compatible with your race."

It is true we are desperate for females ever since the Great Plague decimated our world several cycles ago, killing most of the females and leaving almost all the survivors infertile. But my species treasures and cherishes females. We do not abuse them—at least, we did not until this day. My gaze sweeps the room, and I am ashamed of what has happened. Even though this tragedy was not my Clan's doing, I cannot help but feel responsible.

"I am sorry," I tell Talia's mate. "It was the Wind Clan who attacked to steal the human females. But you are right; there is no excuse for this behavior. I vow that we will help you build a peaceful life on this world. The actions of the Wind Clan will not go unpunished." I train my ears to the lingering sounds of battle still filtering into the med center. "Even now, Varus is fighting them off."

In my hearts, I know I should fly out to help, but I cannot convince myself to leave Talia's side. As far as I could tell while I raced toward the med center, the Fire Clan has gained the upper hand. Varus's guards are among the fiercest warriors of our kind. I do not doubt that they will drive the Wind Clan from their territory.

"We don't want your help," the male grinds out. "You think you can buy us off by offering food and shelter so that you can use our females as breeders?" He shakes his head vehemently. "I've heard about your fated mates, but humans don't feel this bond and you can't convince us to go along with it. Lilliana may have been fooled by Prince Varus, but the rest of us will not be."

"Stop," Talia interjects. "Varus has been nothing but kind to us. His Clan has saved us from the desert and offered us a place to live. And Llyr," she points to me, "saved me, Milo. I would have died if he hadn't caught me when I fell."

I cannot believe how fervently she defends me to her mate. I thought she would hold my kind responsible for the injuries suffered by all her people this day.

Rakan—Varus's guard—moves to my side, interrupting my thoughts. His red eyes meet mine evenly as his orange scales darken with anger. "Prince Llyr, it is Raidyn's cousin who is responsible for the attack. Prince Raidyn has now defeated him and forced the Wind Clan to stand down. Varus is asking for your help to make sure the fighting does not begin anew."

I dart a glance at Talia and her mate before nodding. I cannot refuse such a request—especially one from the prince of this land. Reluctantly, I move to leave her side, but her small hand on my forearm stops me abruptly.

Talia lifts her gaze to me, her blue eyes meeting mine full of worry. "Be careful, Llyr."

Her concern touches me. Deeply. "I will."

Off to the side I notice Milo glaring at me, and my hearts clench in my chest. She is not mine. She is his, and I have no choice but to accept it.

CHAPTER 6

TALIA

My mind slowly trickles back into awareness at the sound of my brother's voice nearby. Ranas was right. His healing fire made me so tired, I fell asleep right after Llyr left.

I open my eyes but then squint at the bright light filtering down from the ceiling overhead. All around me, the med center is a hive of activity. Healers and medics move among the rows of beds, filled with patients—both Drakarian and human.

The crisp scent of antiseptic in the air and the stark white walls remind me a bit of the med center on the ship. I try to turn on my side toward the sound of my brother's voice, but stop as a sharp stab of pain moves through my body.

Everything hurts, and I feel like I'm dying. The pain is so bad I can hardly stand it. When Ranas treated me with his healing fire, it took the raw edge off my initial pain. It even lulled me into a light sleep for a bit, but a constant, terrible throb plagues my side now that I'm awake again. Don't these Drakarians know anything about pain relievers?

Healer Ranas walks up beside my brother.

"Where's Anna?" She's a doctor. Surely, she can help me. I scan the room but don't see her anywhere. Oh Stars, I hope she's all right. In all the commotion, I didn't even think to look for her earlier.

Milo takes my hand. "Anna's fine. She came by while you were sleeping to check on you."

"What about the others?" I grip Healer Ranas's forearm. "Please. Tell me. Is everyone all right? Is the fighting over?"

He nods. "The battle is over. All the humans are accounted for and being treated. All should recover."

I think of Llyr and the other Drakarians who came to our aid. "What about your people?"

He meets my gaze evenly, something akin to guilt flashing across his eyes. "You are concerned for their welfare even after what happened?"

I nod. "I can't hold all of you responsible for what the Wind Clan did."

Milo crosses his arms and rolls his eyes. "Maybe *you* can't," he mutters.

I shoot him a pointed look. "Go check on everyone else. Let me know how they're doing."

Reluctantly, he leaves. I'm glad; I don't like his sour attitude. There are good and bad people on this planet, just like on the colony ships. He shouldn't judge all the Drakarians based on the actions of a few.

I meet Ranas's eyes evenly. "I know it was the Wind Clan who tried to take us. The rest of your people have gone out of their way to help mine."

His smile is faint. "Lie back so I can treat your injuries again with my healing fire."

I've heard a lot about their healing fire but never saw it in action until today. Only Earth Clan Drakarians possess this ability; that's why they are known as the Healing Clan.

"I will do as much as I can, but I must reserve some of my energy to treat the other females. I've sent for more of my Clan to help treat the wounded," he adds. "Some have already arrived and more are on their way."

I bite back a groan of frustration that this second round of treatment won't heal me completely. Fortunately, however, my pain is so much less now than it initially was, so I'm not going to complain.

I scan the room and notice several other people—humans and Drakarians—whose injuries are far worse than mine. So I understand why Ranas needs to save some of his energy to heal the rest while we wait for more Healers to arrive.

Leaning over, he takes a deep breath and opens his mouth. A blue-green flame forms and gently blows over my wounds. His breath is merely warm across my skin. It's comforting in a way that I never expected it could be. Closing my eyes, I can imagine being wrapped in a huge, fluffy blanket as he works, the flame like a soothing balm over my injuries.

When Ranas is finished, he apologizes again for not being able to do more, then moves on to the next patient. Truthfully, he did more already than I could have hoped. His healing fire is impressive.

I stare at the ceiling as I wait for Milo to report back on our friends' condition. I hope they're okay. As if my very thoughts have summoned them, Lilly and Skye enter the room.

I'm so excited to see Skye that I jerk upright in bed. I hiss as pain shoots through my body. The ache is no longer unbearable, but it hurts nonetheless.

"Be careful." She smiles, her blue eyes dancing with happiness. "You're still healing."

Despite my pain, I stand and pull Skye into a hug, running my hand over her long, silken blond hair. I'm so happy; I can't believe she's finally here. "I'm so glad you're all right. We were worried about you. What happened?"

She opens her mouth to speak but trails off as my eyes fly wide. A tall Drakarian with light-gray scales approaches behind her. His ice blue gaze meets mine and panic stops my heart. He's a member of the Wind Clan. "Skye, look out!"

She puts her hands up in a placating gesture. "It's all right," she hastily reassures me. "You don't have to worry. It's just Raidyn. He's not a threat."

As my gaze rakes over his form, I note the long, jagged scar that runs from the top of his left brow down to his cheek.

I gasp. "What do you mean, he's not a threat? That scar." I point animatedly to his face, remembering how John described the dragon who attacked them. "He's the one who stole you away, isn't he?"

Skye takes his hand, standing tall. "Prince Raidyn is my husband. Er… mate, I mean," she corrects herself.

Only now do I notice the brightly glowing fate mark pattern on his chest. My mouth drifts open as I blink. "You two?" I ask in disbelief. "You're fated like Lilly and Varus?"

Skye nods and smiles up at her mate. His stoic expression softens as he regards her like she's a goddess—the same way Varus looks at Lilly. She steps forward. "Not all of the Wind Clan is evil, Talia. Raidyn and his father—the former king—had a… falling out."

Her tone implies there's more to the story, but I quietly wait for her to explain what exactly happened to her and how she found us.

She continues. "Raidyn's cousin manipulated Raidyn's

dad. He ordered the attack on the Fire Clan to steal us humans. But Raidyn defeated him"—she looks up and smiles again at her mate—"and became the new king of the Wind Clan."

My brow furrows in confusion. "So that means… you're a queen now?"

Raidyn wraps a possessive arm around her shoulders and tugs her against him. "Yes," he says proudly. "Skye is my mate and queen to our people."

Sadness seeps into my heart as I realize what this means. If she's queen of the Wind Clan, she'll be expected to live there with her new mate. "So you're leaving again, aren't you?"

She takes my hand and gives it a reassuring squeeze. "We can still visit one another, you know."

"Can we?" I wonder how these politics will play out. Sure, King Raidyn might be one of the good guys, but I can't just forget what the rest of his people tried to do. Even though they acted on a different king's orders, shouldn't the Wind warriors have realized that kidnapping is wrong?

I look Raidyn up and down, still not sure if I'm ready to like him. "I mean… aren't relations kind of tense now that your people attacked another Clan?" I reluctantly finish.

Skye frowns and Raidyn's expression grows guilty. I didn't want to point it out, but it had to be said. I was sure I would be taken and forced into a life of slavery. So convinced that I jumped off a dragon's back because I'd rather die than end up like that.

Raidyn meets my eyes evenly. "I vow that the males who participated in this attack will be punished. I am ashamed my Clan did this to your people. But I assure you that your friend is safe with me and will be protected at all times in my territory. I would never let harm befall her. She is my fated one—my linaya—and I will guard her with my life."

He sounds so sincere. The complete knight-in-shining-armor package standing before me, declaring his love and devotion for my friend, just like Varus does with Lilly. When these dragon-men find their fated one, they fall quickly and they fall hard.

Out of the corner of my eye, I notice a figure freeze in the doorway. I glance over Skye's shoulder to find John. His jaw drops, and he stares at her as if he's seen a ghost.

Skye and Raidyn follow my line of sight. The moment Raidyn's eyes meet John's, he growls menacingly. The sound fills my veins with ice.

"You!" Raidyn hisses through gritted teeth. "You hurt my linaya. You tried to force-mate her."

John's eyes are full of fear as he turns to run. He trips over his feet and falls back. As soon as he hits the ground, he crab-crawls backward as Raidyn stalks toward him. "Wait! I can explain!" he wails. "Please don't kill me!"

Raidyn rushes toward him with inhuman speed. Grabbing his collar, he hauls John off the floor, holding him up with one hand as if he weighs nothing.

John kicks at the air, flailing wildly in Raidyn's grasp. "Let me go! Please! Don't kill me!"

Raidyn's eyes burn with rage as he bares his sharp fangs and releases a low, threatening growl. "You should be dead. You will die for daring to harm my mate," he grinds out. "My vow."

"Stop!" Varus calls from across the room. "What is the meaning of this?"

Skye steps between Raidyn and Varus. "John attacked me when we were alone together, searching for Lilly. If Raidyn hadn't come along, he might have—" Her blue eyes are bright with tears as her breath hitches in her throat.

Raidyn finishes her sentence. "He tried to force-mate her,

Varus. I witnessed his crime with my own eyes. He deserves death."

My mouth drifts open in shock. John is many things, but a rapist? I didn't think he was capable of that. Suddenly, all his hesitation when Varus questioned him makes sense.

"Set him down," Varus commands Raidyn.

Reluctantly, he obeys, releasing his grip and allowing John to drop like a stone to the floor at his feet.

"Is this truth?" Varus glares at John.

John's eyes are wide with fear as he stares at Varus. "I—I," he stumbles over his words. "She wanted it. She's the one who came on to me!"

Skye gives him a thunderous look. "I told you 'no' several times, but you wouldn't listen," she hisses as she stalks toward him. "How dare you lie about what you did! What would you have done after you'd raped me—killed me? Left me to die? You disgust me."

Varus and Raidyn both snarl.

Without warning, John pulls a blaster from his belt and points it at Skye. "Yeah," he sneers. "That's exactly what I would have done. And now, we can die together."

A bright flash of light arcs from the barrel. The world shifts into slow-motion as Raidyn spreads his dark gray wings wide to shield her. The beam tears through his sail, and I jump up, pushing Skye out of the way.

Pain explodes across my torso when the shot hits my side.

I collapse to the floor in a crumpled heap, curling into myself as I grit my teeth in agony. A flurry of chaos erupts all around me. I blink at the ceiling as the world begins to tilt and spin, barely registering Llyr's panicked silver eyes that hover overhead.

He drops to his knees and gathers me to his chest. "Talia!"

I reach a trembling hand up to touch his cheek. "Llyr," I barely manage.

"I'm here," He lifts his gaze, frantically scanning the room. "We need the Healer!" He looks back down at me, cupping my face. "I'm here, my beloved."

Unable to stay conscious, I close my eyes and fall away into darkness.

CHAPTER 7

LLYR

I watch, frozen, as the blast hits Talia and she crumples to the floor.

Raidyn's injury, though painful, can be easily repaired by the Healers. But Talia is human. Her body is smaller and more fragile than a Drakarian. I do not know how badly the blast could harm a member of her species. Her blue eyes are fixed on the ceiling, her eyelids fluttering as she struggles to remain conscious. The sight strikes fear in my hearts.

I drop to my knees and gather her in my arms. Crimson blood seeps through the white fabric of her robe at the site of her injury, filling me with panic. "Talia!"

She reaches up and lightly touches my cheek. "Llyr," she whispers.

I brush the hair back from her face as I hold her tightly to me. "I'm here." Frantic, I scan the room and cry out, "We need a Healer!" I look back down and cup her face. "I'm here, my beloved."

Panic constricts my chest as she closes her eyes and goes limp in my arms.

"I'm here." Her friend Anna drops to her knees beside me. Her green eyes staring down at her friend with unmistakable panic as she presses her hands to the wound, trying to stop the bleeding. Healer Ranas rushes to her side to aid her.

Despite his wound, Raidyn releases a feral roar and lunges for John.

The male raises the blaster to fire at him again, but Raidyn knocks the weapon from his grasp and swipes at his throat with his claws.

Blood spurts from John's neck as he grasps futilely at the mortal wound. He releases a choked gasp and collapses to the ground. A crimson pool forms around his body as the light slowly fades from his eyes.

Several of the humans look away, their faces twisted in disgust and horror. Varus's mate, Lilliana, hovers nearby, solely focused on Talia.

Ranas runs the scanner over her body while Anna watches, her long brown hair tied in a loose knot at the nape of her neck. Though she is the only Healer in the human crew, she is still not entirely familiar with our technology, and she certainly does not possess healing fire like the Healers of the Earth Clan.

"Place her back on the bed," Ranas orders me. Fierce protectiveness overtakes me. Talia is mine, and I wish I could kill John all over again to make him pay for what he's done to my mate.

Quickly, I lay her down on the bed.

"Remove that." Ranas gestures to her robes.

Her mate stands nearby but makes no move to assist, so I extend my claws and tear the fabric from her body to expose the open wound. I struggle to bite back my frustration at Milo. How could Talia choose such a useless mate?

Red blood pools in the sheets below the side of her torso, filling me with dread. "Will she—"

I stop short. I cannot bring myself to finish my question because if Ranas tells me that she will not survive, I do not believe I will, either. Even though she is not technically my mate, every instinct screams that she is mine.

My hearts and soul are already irrevocably bound to hers. Fear winds around my spine at the thought of losing her to this injury.

Anna watches wide-eyed as Ranas begins to breathe his healing fire over her wound. The green flame does not burn like regular fire or my frostfire, so it must be a strange sight to behold for a human. I notice Ranas's flames do not glow as brightly as they normally do, his power diminished by overuse and exhaustion.

Talia's tissue begins to knit back together, but when Ranas's eyes meet mine, I recognize his fatigue. He stops, sending me a sorrowful look. His gaze drifts down to my chest, and I clench my jaw in frustration because I know he searches again for the fate mark.

"I have used up most of my energy healing the others," he explains. "I am unable to mend this wound completely for now. But I promise you, my friend, she will live."

Despite his reassurance, I struggle to contain the low growl rising in my throat. "You cannot leave her like this. She needs—"

I begin to snarl, but he raises a hand in a plea to allow him to continue.

"I have sent word to my Clan. A few of the Healers have already arrived and many more are on the way. They should be entering the medical center shortly."

When I look over his shoulder, I note several new faces walking from bed to bed, treating the injured. These must be the Healers who have recently arrived. I'm glad when I notice

Prince Kaj of the Earth Clan making his way toward us. His green scales are slightly darkened with anger as he looks at all the injured before him. His golden eyes meet mine, and I know we are of the same mind in this regard—both of us enraged that such a terrible thing has happened this day. He is as skilled a Healer as Ranas, and I'm sure he'll be able to save my linaya.

Talia's mate scoots closer to her side. He gives me a hesitant look, and it is almost as if I can see the inner workings of his mind playing out across his expression.

He does not like me, but that is to be expected. Here I stand, holding his mate's hand as if he is not even here. She is not mine, and I have no right to touch her, but I refuse to let go.

I vow that when she recovers, I will confess my feelings in an attempt to persuade her to become my mate. If Milo were worthy of her, I would not even consider such a dishonorable tactic. But I have seen enough to know that he will not care for her as well as I could.

Her condition appears to have shaken him so much that he says nothing, probably remembering how she chastised him for his rude remarks to me earlier.

Anna lifts her gaze to us. "She'll probably sleep for a few hours. It seems like healing fire causes drowsiness in us humans." She smiles kindly. "You're the one who saved her, right?"

I nod. She darts a glance at Milo.

"What?" He frowns, his blue eyes narrowed slightly. "Why are you looking at me like that?"

"Prince Llyr saved your sister. The polite response would be to thank him, Milo," she comments pointedly.

Sister?

I freeze, my mind racing.

I should have seen it before. The same blue eyes, light

52

skin, and dark brown hair. How could I have missed the similarities? I was such a fool to assume this male was her mate. Now that I know he is not, hope fills me anew.

"Thanks for saving Talia," he grumbles.

With a slightly clenched jaw, I lower my gaze. I am ashamed of my people's behavior this day. "I am sorry for what the Wind Clan has done. It is not our way."

He huffs out a frustrated sigh and rolls his eyes. "Not your way?" He gestures toward the exit and the city beyond. "I just witnessed an epic dragon battle that suggests otherwise."

He is right. The Wind Clan tried to take the females against their will. I place a hand to my chest "I promise you that my Clan will do everything in our power to make sure no such crime is committed ever again."

He crosses his arms over his chest and sits back as he levels me with a glare. "We'll see about that."

Although his answer distresses me somewhat, I must admire his bravery. He is no match for a Drakarian, and yet, he openly defies one to protect his sister from what he perceives to be a threat to her wellbeing. I hold his gaze for a moment but say nothing. I suppose, if our positions were reversed, I would feel the same. Besides, if he is to be my family soon, I do not wish to anger him further. My mate would surely wish for us to get along.

"Llyr?" Varus calls behind me. "I need to speak with you."

I'm reluctant to leave my mate but am comforted that she is not alone. Her brother will remain at her side.

I turn to Varus. Raidyn stands beside him, his torn wing already healed.

With a heavy sigh, I gently squeeze Talia's hand and reach out to brush the hair back from her face. I lift my eyes to her brother as I stand to leave. "I will return shortly."

"I'll bet," he grumbles, and I cannot help but notice the

sarcasm laced in his tone. It bothers me. I do not want a rift between us. I must find a way to remedy this at once. And the best way to discover this is to speak with Varus and Raidyn and their human mates.

I wonder whether their fate marks appeared instantly. I've heard that recognizing the bond by sight does not always mean the mark appears right away. Moreover, I am eager to learn what I can about the experience of Prince Varus and Raidyn regarding their linayas.

CHAPTER 8

TALIA

My mind slowly returns to awareness as warm air blows gently across my torso, easing the dull ache in my side. I open my eyes to find a Healer standing over me. The beautiful emerald coloring of his scales designates him as a member of the Earth Clan. I stare in wonder at the blue-green healing flame licking at my skin around the site of my injury. This ability is nothing short of a miracle. My pain slowly ebbs away as the torn tissue begins to knit back together before my eyes.

As if sensing my thoughts, the Healer lifts his gaze to mine, a hint of a smile curving his lips. "You find our healing abilities strange."

Although his inflection does not change, I understand he is asking a question. "Yes. But helpful," I add with a grin.

He dips his chin in a subtle nod. "That it is." He darts a glance at my injury. "I am told your species takes longer to heal than mine. This should be healed completely by tomorrow. If you need any further assistance, please let me know. I am Prince Kaj of the Earth Clan."

I sit up, wincing slightly. "Thank you, Prince Kaj."

"What is wrong?" Llyr approaches behind Kaj, his face a mask of concern. "Are you all right?"

"Yes, just a bit sore. That's all."

Despite my words, Llyr turns to Kaj with a muted growl. "She is obviously still in pain. Why have you not treated her?"

Kaj purses his lips while a hint of irritation shifts into his gaze. "I assure you, Prince Llyr, I have already seen to her injury, but her people do not heal as quickly as ours. That is the cause of her residual pain. Tomorrow, she should be completely healed."

"That's not good enough," Llyr snaps. "You—"

I cut him off abruptly. "Llyr, stop."

His gaze sweeps to mine and his expression softens. I'm touched by his concern, but the aggression is completely unnecessary. "I'm fine, Llyr. I swear."

"But you are still hurting," he protests. "You should not be in pain."

I shrug. "It's not that bad. I feel much better than I did earlier. In fact," I shift and hang my legs over the bed, "I think I'd like to take a walk. Stretch my muscles a bit."

Both Llyr and Kaj blink slowly, looking astonished. "You should rest," Kaj insists.

I roll my eyes. "Look, I know you think all humans are pitiful weaklings, but we're not that fragile. I'd like to move around a bit, get my blood flowing again."

He frowns. "Fine. But someone should escort you, just in case."

I turn my head, scanning the room for my brother or one of my friends, but I don't see anyone.

As if sensing my disappointment, Llyr's eyes meet mine.

"Your brother went looking for something to eat. I would gladly accompany you, if you'd like."

I swallow nervously as a warm flush creeps across my cheeks. Despite his grumbly attitude toward Kaj just a second ago, Llyr is a sweet guy. I'm completely in love with him, even though I shouldn't be. "All right. That sounds nice."

His lips curve into a heart-stopping smile. It takes me a moment to remember myself. He tips his head to the side, but I stand and grin nervously. "All right. Where are we going?"

His brow furrows. "Where would you like to go?"

CHAPTER 9

LLYR

While I wait for Talia's answer, I turn to Kaj, hoping to apologize for my rude behavior. My jaw drops when I notice the bright, glowing pattern of the fate mark across his chest.

His eyes meet mine.

"Who is it?" I ask.

He scans the room and closes his eyes, drawing in a deep breath. "She is near," he whispers, more to himself than to me. "I can sense it."

With that, he walks away as if in a trance. I do not call him back, for I understand this feeling. I am completely enthralled with Talia. When I turn back to her, I find her eyes tracking Kaj as he crosses the room to speak to another human female. She sighs heavily and shakes her head.

I cock my head to the side. "What is wrong?"

"I just don't understand all this fate bond stuff." She lifts her gaze to mine. "I mean, what about just getting to know someone and falling in love that way? Wouldn't it be a lot easier?"

Her words trouble me and I frown. "You dislike the idea of the fate bond?"

She opens her mouth to answer, but Lilliana approaches, her face lit by a smile. "Varus and I ordered several rooms made ready for all of you to stay in the castle."

Talia nods. "Thanks. I just need to swing by my apartment. If it's still somewhat intact, I can pick up a few belongings."

Lilliana's expression falls. "Milo and a few of the others already went back there but there's not much left after the attack."

It pains me to see my linaya's distress at her words. My hands curl into fists at my side as I think again of the Wind Clan. Curse them for their dishonorable actions. I cannot believe their warriors did this. Even though the order came from their sovereign, I cannot believe they blindly followed the king's lead.

"Thank goodness you're married to the Fire Clan prince, right?" Talia offers her friend a pained smile. "If not for that, we'd have no place to stay."

Lilliana takes her hand. "You've always been welcome to stay with us. You're like a sister to me, Talia."

"Thanks."

Varus joins his mate and pulls her back into his arms. He presses a tender kiss to the top of her head and she smiles up at him.

They look so happy, he and his human female. A sharp pang of jealousy stabs me as I glance at my chest once again. Why has the fate mark still not revealed itself? I know in my hearts that Talia is mine. I merely need the mark to confirm it.

Lilliana looks back at Talia. "We're going to talk to a few people, but I'll see you in the castle later, all right?"

Talia nods and then turns to me. "You still up for that walk?"

I study her in concern. The medical center is not very far from the castle, but she is still healing. "Is it wise for you to do this in your current condition?"

She grins. "Really, Llyr, you act like humans are so fragile, but we're not."

In her eyes, I can see the truth. She truly believes she is strong. However, I know better. Her species is physically much weaker than mine, and the shock of this day's attack still fills me with fear. An involuntary shudder runs through my body. I could have lost her so easily.

I scan her form as I consider other options. An excursion that will satisfy her without taxing her injured body too much. "How about I fly us to the castle, and then we can stroll through the palace courtyard and gardens?"

She hesitates. "I—I'm not sure I want to fly just yet."

My hearts clench. "Forgive me. Of course, you would not wish to fly." I nod, resolute. "We shall walk, then."

A faint smile curves her lips.

Together, we start toward the castle. We're not even halfway across the large courtyard when her frail hand on my forearm halts my steps. I turn to her, scanning her face.

"I just need a moment," she says. I notice her arm is braced across her torso as she breathes through pursed lips. I remember Kaj explaining that the tissue has not fully healed. She pushes her physical limits too far for my liking.

I consider her for a moment then make an offer. "I can fly you the rest of the way in this form, holding you in my arms instead of changing to my draka form and placing you on my back. Would this be agreeable to you?"

Her brow furrows softly while she considers before she

nods. "Why didn't you tell me you could carry me in this form earlier? I would have definitely taken you up on that offer." She smiles. "That slope we just climbed was a killer."

I arch a brow at her. "You did not ask."

She laughs heartily but breaks off, inhaling sharply and banding her arm across her injury. Recovering, she gives me a small grin. "Don't make me laugh right now, all right?"

This, I can do. I've often been told my personality is too somber. My sister is the outgoing one in the family, not me. I smile warmly at her. "As you wish."

My mother has often expressed concern that I will have difficulty finding a female to bond with. When we entertain at the castle, I often put on a false front, trying to be more like my sister whom everyone adores.

Being here in the Fire Clan territory, I have observed Varus rather closely. He is very charismatic. People are drawn to him because of his outgoing nature. I envy him how easily he makes friends and puts people at ease with his disarming personality.

I worried, at first, that Talia would want me to be more like him. That she would find me too serious and boring. I was surprised when she sought me out a few days ago to walk with her in the palace gardens. She even told me that she enjoyed my company.

With her, I am able to be myself. She accepts me for who I am and does not judge me harshly for my quiet and pensive nature.

She lifts her blue eyes to mine, and I am completely enchanted as she smiles up at me.

Carefully, I lean forward and place one hand behind her back and another under her knees to lift her into my arms. I pull her against my chest and make certain I have a secure hold on her before we lift off. She is precious to me and I take great care to ensure she is safe.

I'm surprised when the normally pink coloring of her cheeks and the bridge of her nose deepens to red.

Strangely, humans can change their skin tone. A female Drakarian's scales will darken when she is aroused, which is also how she would signal interest in forming a bond with a male.

I wonder if it is the same with Talia's species. Is this how humans attract a mate? I've witnessed Lilliana's face darken around her mate, Varus. Talia's color changes often, but I have never had the opportunity to ask what it means.

"Your face has changed color," I tell her. "Are all humans capable of this?"

Her sparkling blue eyes snap up to meet mine and I watch with a frown as the redness of her cheeks brightens even more. "Uh, I, uh… yes," she finally answers.

I cock my head to the side as I study her, hoping that I have correctly guessed that she desires me. "What does it mean?"

"It happens when we're nervous, or," she lowers her gaze and drops her voice to barely a whisper, "attracted to someone."

I freeze. My hearts begin hammering in my chest. "And what is the reason you change colors now?" I ask, both anxious and fearful in equal measure for her answer.

Is she nervous because we are about to fly? Or is she attracted to me? I send a silent prayer to the gods that she answers the latter.

With her gaze still lowered, she murmurs reluctantly, "I guess it's a bit of both." Clearing her throat, she changes the subject. "How long do you think it will take to reach the palace gardens from here?"

My lips curve into a smile as happiness blooms in my chest. She finds me attractive. Tilting my chin up, I regard the palace. "No time at all," I tell her then spread my wings wide and lift off.

She yelps in surprise, tightening her arms around my neck. "Don't drop me!"

"I would never let you fall, Talia. My vow," I reply. She rewards me with her brilliant smile.

Catching the wind in my sails, I ascend, leaving the buildings and streets behind. I bank in a wide arc over the mesa as she stares in wonder at the city below. When we reach the castle, I circle once to afford her a better view from above before gently gliding down to the courtyard.

As soon as I place her feet on the ground, she turns to me, her eyes sparkling with joy. "That was amazing."

I bow slightly. "I am glad you thought so."

"Want to walk with me in the gardens?"

"You are not tired?"

"No." She grins. "Not anymore."

In truth, I am glad she does not require further rest. I long to spend more time with her, especially since my sister and I will be leaving tomorrow.

Several alima stones light the pathways that weave through the gardens. Although surrounded by desert, the palace courtyard is a lush paradise full of flowering plants and bushes. Long vines trail down the walls, laden with vibrant blossoms in red, purple, blue, and yellow. They sway gently in the breeze like living curtains.

Water is precious in the Fire Clan lands, but I have heard that natural springs flow in the ground below. A small stream winds along our path, and as I watch the bubbling current, I cannot help but miss my home.

"Thank you again for saving me," Talia's soft voice rips me from my thoughts. "I would have died if you hadn't caught me."

The memory of her fall has bothered me and although I

am hesitant to bring up such a traumatic experience, I must understand her actions. I fix her with a steadfast gaze. "I watched you jump off the back of the Wind draka. Why did you do this?"

She turns her gaze to the opposite wall with a faraway look. "I was afraid he would carry me off to become a slave. I thought the Wind Clan might... force-mate us and use us as breeders." Her voice quavers. "And I... I would rather be dead than to live at someone's mercy."

My hearts clench. I reach out to cup her cheek, surprised when she does not pull away from my touch. Her blue eyes, deeper than the ocean, stare up at me. "That will never happen—my vow. Even if the Wind Clan had taken you back to their lands, they would not have force-mated you. It is not our way."

A tear slips down her cheek. "You say that, but you don't know how terrifying that was. Your people..." She shakes her head, trailing off. "Up until then, I'd been treated with nothing but kindness, but now I... I don't know what to think."

I don't allow her to look away. "When I realized that the Wind Clan was attacking, I searched for you, Talia."

Her brow furrows. "You did?"

"Yes." I lift my hands and crook my first two fingers to emphasize my point, using the human gesture of air quotations that she taught me. "I vow that if anyone ever tries to take you against your will, I will find you and I will save you."

A beautiful smile crests her lips as she takes my hands in her own. "Thank you, Llyr. I owe you my life."

"You owe me nothing," I respond confidently.

As she stares up at me, her words from earlier float to the forefront of my mind. I am hesitant to ask, but I know that I must. "We never finished discussing the bond. Do you dislike the idea of a fated mate?"

"Yes."

Her answer surprises me. "Why?"

"Because…" She lifts her gaze to mine and something akin to sadness reflects in her eyes. "It means that no matter how much I might like a Drakarian, I cannot let myself fall in love with him."

I frown, not quite understanding.

She continues. "Unless we are fated, there is always a risk that the man I love could end up fated to someone else. He would never truly be mine."

Drawing in a deep breath, I steel my nerves to give her my truth. "You are my mate. My linaya." I place my open palm to my chest. "I feel it here."

"I don't understand." Her small brow furrows in confusion. "Your chest… you don't have the fate mark like Varus and Raidyn do."

Clenching my jaw, I nod. "It does not always appear right away. We recognize our fated ones by sight first; the mark will come later. I am certain."

Her eyes search mine. "How long have you felt this way?"

"When the Fire Clan brought you and your people out of the desert, I walked into the castle courtyard, feeling as if I were drawn to seek you. My soul recognized yours the moment I saw you there." I take both her hands in mine. "It is why I sought you out the first time we spoke." I drop to my knees before her. "I desire you as my mate, Talia. Please accept me as yours."

She gives me a pained look. "I wish I could, Llyr, but I can't."

My hearts sink. "Why? We are kindred spirits, you and I. I am more certain of that each time we speak. You are attracted to me, are you not?" I reach up to gently brush my fingers across her cheek, watching in wonder as a warm flush follows in their wake. She desires me as much as I do her. Of this, I am certain.

"Yes, but this is more complicated than you think."

"What is it?" I ask. "Do you fear that I will force you to be mine? I would never coerce you, Talia. The choice is yours, whether to accept me or not, regardless of the fate mark. The female is the one who chooses."

"No, Llyr. I just…" She trails off, looking lost. "Without the mark, how can you be sure? I mean, we're two different species."

I lead her hand to my chest, placing her palm between my two hearts. "I am certain because I feel it here. The pull of the bond is strong within me."

"What if you're wrong? What if the pull is not for me?"

"Why would—" I start, but she interrupts.

"What if your fate mark appears someday, but for someone else?"

"That will not happen."

"You don't know that," she argues. "I can't allow myself to fall for you, never knowing if you will end up fated to another person."

I move to reassure her. "I do not *want* anyone else. I only want *you*, Talia."

"What would happen, Llyr, if a Drakarian got married and then the mark appeared on their chest for someone else?"

I shake my head. "I do not know. It has never happened before."

She shoots me a frustrated look. "I can't risk my heart, Llyr. I refuse to take that leap, knowing I could end up broken later."

Is she worried that I may be fated to another human female when we find more of her crew? We've talked many times about the search for other escape pods. Even now, several of our ships scour the system for survivors and patrols scan the planet's surface. I do not believe hers is the only escape pod to survive the attack, but if she is worried that I will be fated to another, I know in my hearts it will not happen.

"You worry for nothing, Talia," I counter. "I know you are mine." I stroke her hands and wrap my tail around her ankle, longing to hold her close.

She stills. Suddenly, she places her hands on my chest, pushing me away. "I'm sorry, Llyr. I just can't."

"Do you love me?" I ask, desperation creeping into my tone.

She looks down. "It doesn't matter."

My hearts stop. "It matters to *me*. Please, Talia. Tell me. Do you love me as I love you?"

Her bottom lip trembles as a tear slips down her cheek. She reaches for my face. "It would be so much easier if—" She cuts off, her gaze dropping to my chest. "If the mark appeared on your scales for me, I would be yours in a heartbeat. But I know that if I let myself fall and things turn out... differently... I would be broken, Llyr. I must protect my heart. I'm protecting us both, Llyr. I'm sorry."

Before I can respond, she turns and heads inside.

"Talia, wait. I—"

"Goodnight, Llyr," she calls without bothering to look back.

Sadness fills me as I watch her walk away. My hearts urge me to run after her, to convince her to be mine. But she does not want me. My gaze drifts to my chest as frustration burns through my veins. Why has the fate mark not appeared? If it had, she would believe me. She would desire me as hers. But without proof that we are fated, she will not even consider becoming mine.

CHAPTER 10

LLYR

Alone in the gardens, I stare up at the sky in despair. The soft crunch of pebbles along the path draws my attention, and I turn to find Varus and Raidyn.

Varus claps a hand on my shoulder. "You appear deep in thought, my friend. What is wrong?"

Sadness and anger war inside me. Many things are wrong. I struggle to restrain a growl at Raidyn. I know it is not his fault that his cousin led the raid to steal the human females, but in truth, I can't help but hold him partly responsible. He knew his father was unfit to rule and should have taken his place on the throne many cycles ago. Because he did not, his father allowed Raidyn's cousin to rule in his stead. This day's battle was the devastating result of that indecision.

"You are angry at me," Raidyn says, and I understand that his statement is also a question.

"Yes," I grind out before I even realize the word has left

my mouth. "Talia is mine, and I almost watched her die this day because of—" I stop just short of laying the entire blame on him.

It is easy to read in his expression that he understands exactly what I meant. "I am sorry, my friend. Truly."

I clench my jaw. "I know it is not your fault." I shake my head as Talia's image floats to the surface of my mind. "Forgive me. I am not quite myself."

Varus lowers his eyes to my chest, and he frowns. "You are certain she is yours?"

"Yes, I am," I confirm. "I have no doubt she is mine."

"Have you told her?" Raidyn asks.

With a heavy sigh, I nod. "Without the mark, she does not believe me. And when I tried to convince her, she pushed me away."

Prince Kaj of the Earth Clan joins us in the garden. Raidyn and Varus both nod in greeting. My gaze immediately finds his chest and the swirling pattern of the fate mark across his scales. I grind my teeth. Why must mine stay hidden?

"They do not recognize the bond like we do." Raidyn's voice pulls me from my thoughts. "It was the same for Skye and me."

"The same was true with Lilliana," Varus adds. "Her species do not have fate bonds. You must be patient." His eyes shift to Raidyn. "Unlike this one."

Raidyn frowns. "I *was* patient with my mate."

Varus rolls his eyes. "Then perhaps Skye was speaking of another male when she told Lilliana about your time together. She told my mate that you insisted she was yours from the first moment you met. That hardly counts as being patient."

Raidyn's expression turns thunderous. "I did not force her to accept me, if that is what you are implying."

Varus laughs. "No, I am merely stating that you wore her down with your insistence that she was your mate." He smirks. "And eventually, she accepted."

"I did not *wear her down*," he growls. "I wooed her."

Varus claps a hand on Raidyn's shoulder with a teasing grin. "Do not be angry with me, my friend. I am merely speaking truth."

Raidyn narrows his eyes, and Varus laughs even louder.

I am glad to see them on friendly terms once more. As fledglings, they were as close as brothers and I hope they can be again. Peace between the four Clans at large would heal our world.

After a moment, Varus's expression sobers. "When do you leave?" he asks Raidyn.

"As soon as possible. After all the damage done by my family, I must make sure order is restored to my kingdom." He pauses. "I do not know if Skye will wish to come with me since the Wind Clan is in so much turmoil."

I stare at him in astonishment, for I understand the implication behind his words. He would leave his mate here for her safety. While I appreciate his concern, I do not know if I could ever part from Talia if she had already accepted me— even for only a short while.

Varus, it seems, understands this as well. He addresses Raidyn. "If she chooses to stay behind, we will keep her safe. My vow."

My thoughts return to Talia. In truth, I will be leaving her behind as well when I return home. Desperate to remain near her, an idea forms in my mind; I must simply convince my friends to agree to help.

Determined, I step forward and face Raidyn. "With your kingdom in turmoil, you will need the support of the other Clans, will you not?"

"What are you suggesting?" Raidyn narrows his eyes. "That I am unfit to rule?"

"No, I am merely stating that together, we are stronger. I'm certain you both remember the days long past when all Clans gathered once every cycle to celebrate the peace between the four Clans." I pause, allowing my words to sink in. "I wish that we could see those days again. Do you not?"

Understanding dawns across their features as each nods in response.

Kaj's golden eyes meet mine briefly before he turns to Varus and Raidyn. "I believe that would be a wise decision."

It has been many cycles since our Clans have gathered in peace. That the four of us are all standing here together is a miracle, considering how much infighting has torn our Clans apart in recent cycles.

I study Prince Kaj. He is a good male, and as my gaze drops again to the swirling fate mark pattern glowing across his green chest, I wish him well. It is wrong to envy another's good fortune. I do not know which female he is bound to, but I suspect it is Talia's friend, Anna. They both practice medicine and it did not escape me how closely he hovered by her side this day.

Only his people—the Earth Clan—have always remained neutral. Sometimes they have been called upon to moderate disputes between the other Clans. That is why Kaj's words hold more weight in this discussion; his support of my suggestion means that Varus and Raidyn will likely accept as well.

Kaj allows his gaze to drift over the three of us before turning his attention back to me. "If I remember correctly, the Water Clan was scheduled to host the next celebration before the practice ended cycles ago. Is that not correct?"

A smile crests my lips, for he is right. My hearts fill with hope. If the celebration is held in my kingdom and the humans attend, Talia will visit my home. She told me she desires to see the ocean. I will still have a chance to pursue her, then.

Perhaps the mark will make itself known at the gathering. Everything would become much simpler if the confirmation of my feelings glowed on the scales between my hearts for the object of my affections to see.

I bow in acknowledgment to Kaj. "My Clan would be honored to host the revived gathering."

"Once there, we could discuss how best to acclimate the humans to our world," Varus adds.

My brow furrows. "What do you mean?"

"At heart, the humans are explorers," he explains. "They set out from their world on colony ships in search of a paradise planet."

"Which is what, exactly?" Kaj asks.

Raidyn darts a glance at Varus before turning his attention back to the group. "My mate, Skye, said their crew was searching for a place with plentiful water and life."

Now I understand why he first looked to Varus. Although the Fire Clan was first to take in the humans, it seems his lands do not fit the environment they were hoping to settle in.

I pity my friend, but I understand how his territory could be considered lacking to the humans. The desert landscape is harsh and unyielding, which is why I was so distraught when my sister agreed to become Varus's mate before he found his linaya. She would not have thrived in such a dry and barren place.

Raidyn continues. "But each of our territories presents different challenges for a human. The Fire territory is dry and lacking in vegetation. The Wind territory, despite its hospitable climate, is built on a series of floating islands. The Earth territory is mountainous, covered in thick jungle, and your dwellings are built on towering mountains. The Water territory," he glances at me, "is mostly ocean, and during the winter, mostly ice. The humans are wingless—they cannot move about as freely as our kind can."

He is right. Although I am reluctant to admit it, despite its harsh climate, Varus's lands are more suited to wingless residents than the rest of our territories. I face him. "Despite lacking the 'paradise' that the humans crave, your cities can easily be modified to accommodate their needs."

I remember that Talia is working with Fire Clan engineers to make the capital more accessible to humans. "I understand that you have already made plans to construct a series of lifts and bridges so that the human crew can move about without relying on Drakarians."

Kaj interjects, "The same could be done in my lands."

His eager words confirm my suspicion that his fated one must be human. My eyes are drawn to his chest and the dimly glowing pattern of the fate mark on his scales. "Who is the one you are drawn to?"

He sighs heavily. "Their Healer. Anna."

From his defeated expression, I can already guess his answer, but I ask anyway. "Has she accepted you?"

He clenches his jaw and shakes his head. At this moment, I feel as if we are two kindred spirits, each longing to be claimed by our mates. At least *he* has the mark, I think to myself bitterly.

I run my hand absently across my chest. Even though my mark is hidden, I will not give up on Talia. I must simply try harder to convince her to be mine and show her that I would be a good mate and provider for our future fledglings.

CHAPTER 11

TALIA

Morning light filters into the room, suffusing the space with a soft, orange glow. Lilly called this a "guest room," but it's palatial by any standards. The large floating bed and thick, red comforter was so soft, I felt like I slept on a cloud. The cleansing room with the sunken pool that could easily fit four people is amazing. Soaking in the warm water was a luxurious decadence unlike anything I've ever experienced before.

If I'm being entirely honest with myself, I'm going to miss these accommodations when the Fire Clan sets us up in new apartments after they repair all the damage that was done to the city.

My gaze drifts to the balcony and the long, sheer red curtains that sway gently in the dry breeze. I'm surprised by the cool morning air that floats in, a remnant of the desert night.

Midday is an entirely different matter, however. It's so hot during the afternoon that I often peel off the layers of fabric I put on just a few hours earlier to keep me warm—only to pull them all back on in the evening.

Drakarians don't seem to share this concern; they hardly wear clothes at all. These aliens aren't ashamed of nudity in the least. Lilly told me they can't shift into their *draka* forms without shredding their clothing. However, they respect that humans prefer not to walk around nude, so Varus has ordered the tailors to make each of us an array of outfits consisting mostly of robes like his people wear when they choose to be dressed.

As I pull on my robe, I marvel at the impossibly soft and airy material. The fabric reminds me of fine silk. My underwear and bra are made of an almost sheer fabric that feels just as soft against my skin. If this is what I have to wear for the rest of my life, I'm all right with it. It's an improvement over the rough yet durable clothing we used to wear on the ships.

The cool breeze ruffles my long, brown hair as I step onto the balcony. When the chill hits my skin, I decide to pull my thicker robe over this one, though I'm sure I'll probably take it off within a few hours.

I strap my small blaster into the holster wrapped around my right thigh. Milo retrieved the weapon from the rubble of our former apartment. I'd hoped we wouldn't need these when we finally settled on a new world, but after what happened yesterday, I think I'd like to stay armed for now.

I step back inside to comb my hair, studying my reflection in the mirror. My thoughts turn to Llyr. I need to find him and apologize for leaving so abruptly last night. It's not his fault that he doesn't have the fate mark on his chest for me.

I hate the fated mate concept. If he dated me like a human man would, I could easily fall for him. He's just my type, with an air of quiet intelligence. In his eyes, I can almost see the gears of his mind constantly turning. He's thoughtful and achingly handsome.

I sigh heavily. None of the other Drakarian males can rival his divine features. I could easily lose myself in his silver eyes. His blue scales remind me of the images of the pure seas on Earth that used to transfix me—before the oceans were carelessly polluted to a thick, muddy brown.

Everything about him draws me in. When I spend time with him, our conversation flows so smoothly. Time seems to fly by when we're together because I enjoy his company so much.

Shaking my head, I try to clear my wandering thoughts. No matter how much I like him, I cannot fall in love. If he wakes one day fated to someone else, it would destroy me.

Despite my conviction, I hate the way I behaved last night. How quickly I shot Llyr down when he asked me to be his. I've always played it safe, never growing close to anyone but my friends and my family. I saw what the other women on the ship went through—seemingly endless cycles of dating followed by rejection and heartbreak. I didn't want to experience that misery. I wanted to find one guy, fall in love, and settle down.

When we joined the Fire Clan and I found out about the fate mark, I was excited—at first. Once I got to know Llyr, I realized how awful the bond truly is. Even if I fall in love with a Drakarian, there is always a risk that he will find his fated one elsewhere. I refuse to take that risk. If I choose Llyr, I want to know our love will last forever.

When I met his eyes last night, I saw the truth. He truly believes I am his *linaya*. Kneeling before me, he regarded me like a rare and precious treasure—a lifetime partner. I wanted nothing more than to wrap my arms around him and tell him that I'm his. That I accept him. But I'm scared he's wrong and I'm not his *linaya*.

Even so, I shouldn't have hurt him. I need to find him and apologize. I know exactly where his room is located, so I decide to head there, hoping to catch him before he starts his day.

When I reach his rooms, I knock on the door. My heart pounds as I wait for an answer. Despite my best intentions, a fantasy of Llyr opening the door, gathering me in his arms, and pressing his lips to mine fills my mind. I want him so much.

I release a frustrated huff. Lilly and Skye are a bad influence. They read too many romance novels and filled my head with idealistic notions of heroes who are too perfect to ever be real. And yet, I suspect the two Drakarians they have mated meet this standard—one that human men could never achieve.

And I suspect that Llyr would more than meet my lofty expectations, if only he were truly mine.

After a while, he still doesn't answer the door, so I decide to go downstairs. I've probably missed him this morning. After all, he's usually talking to Varus or his sister, Noralla, in the gardens.

My mind replays our conversation last night as I make my way to the courtyard. Doubt and indecision begin to creep in. Maybe I should just take the risk, tell him that I want him, and see what happens. He's leaving soon—I don't know when I'll see him again, if ever. I want to get everything out in the open. Maybe… we could give this a try.

I find Lilly smiling warmly in the courtyard. "Good morning," she greets me. "Did you sleep well?"

"Yes," I lie. I hardly slept a wink. I was thinking about Llyr all night long.

"Milo asked about you. I think he's in the kitchen having breakfast. And Skye said to tell you goodbye. She and Raidyn already left for the Wind Clan territory."

"What about Llyr?" I ask. "Do you know where he is?"

Over her shoulder, I notice Varus arch an inquisitive brow as she replies, "He left this morning with his sister."

My heart sinks. "He left? I thought they weren't supposed to leave until tomorrow." I swallow hard against the sudden lump in my throat. What if I never see him again? From what Lilly has told me, it's rare for members of different Clans to visit one another. They mostly keep to themselves and their territories. "Is he coming back?"

She shakes her head. "They're returning to Water Clan territory. Their home."

"Oh," I reply, fighting to hide my disappointment.

It doesn't work; Lilly notices the slight quaver of my voice. She takes my hand to comfort me. "Llyr talked to Varus and Raidyn about the bond. Varus says the fate mark doesn't always show up right away."

I glance at Lilly's mate. "It is truth," he confirms.

I'm desperate to believe him, but there are still too many unknowns. "But we're different species," I counter. "How can you be sure it works the same way for us?"

He lowers his gaze. "I cannot be certain. I only know it is not uncommon for a delay to happen among my people."

Lilly glances over her shoulder at Varus, and something unspoken passes between them. He nods and excuses himself. As soon as he's gone, she turns back to me pointedly. "I know you. You've already fallen for him, haven't you?"

"It doesn't matter, Lilly. He's already gone, and maybe that's for the best. If he had stayed, I'd have a hard time resisting his advances." I lift my gaze to her, pleading for her to understand. "I have to protect my heart."

"But he loves you," she protests, "why would—"

"What if Varus hadn't displayed the fate mark? What if you had fallen for him only to find out that he was meant to be with someone else? How would you feel then?"

Her gaze holds mine for a moment before she finally nods. "You're right. That would have been awful."

"That's why I told Llyr I didn't want him—my heart wouldn't survive that rejection."

"Well, you're going to have to figure out what to do when you see him again."

I frown. "What do you mean? I thought you said he left."

"We're going to the Water Clan territory soon to celebrate peace among the four Clans."

"What?"

She nods. "The Clans used to gather annually in a festival of peace. They've decided to stop their infighting and restart this tradition."

I'm not sure how I feel about this revelation. On the one hand, I do want to see Llyr again. And I am desperate to see the ocean—a real ocean, untainted by trash and pollution like the sea I remember on Earth when I was a child.

On the other hand, I'm afraid to go. If he asks me to be his once more, I don't know that I'll be strong enough to deny him.

CHAPTER 12

LLYR

S tanding on the balcony of my castle, I study the night
sky. The tide is high. The crisp, saline breeze whips
around my form as waves crash against the shoreline
below.

Although it has not been very long, it feels like an eternity
has passed since I left the Fire Clan territory. I sigh as my
thoughts drift to Talia.

I rub my chest, by now an almost instinctive movement.
Why does my mark not appear? I know she is mine just as
surely as I know the sun will rise each morning and the
moon will replace it each night. It is an irrevocable truth that
resonates deep in my soul.

"Are you all right?" Noralla's gentle voice calls me back
from my thoughts.

I turn to watch her approach with a nod. "Yes. I am fine."
The lie brands my tongue.

A faint smile tugs at her mouth. "You forget that I can tell
when you are lying, dear brother."

With a heavy sigh, I meet her eyes evenly. She knows me too well.

"The one you long for will be here tomorrow, along with the other humans," she offers. "Perhaps then, she might—"

I clench my jaw as I shake my head, cutting her off. "Without the mark, she does not want me. She fears that I am mistaken, that she is not my linaya. She worries that my mark will appear for another."

"Ah." Noralla nods, understanding dawning on her features. "This means she already returns your feelings."

My eyes snap up to meet hers. "What makes you believe that?"

"Really, Brother," she chastises me with an affectionate chuckle. "The hearts are fragile things where matters of love are concerned. She pushes you away to protect hers." She studies me curiously. "Can you not see it?"

I blink slowly, mulling over the meaning of her words. Hope fills me anew, along with a heavy dose of renewed determination. "When she arrives for the celebration, I will make certain she knows that I love her. I will prove that I am hers and hers alone. I will woo her and show her that I do not need the mark to confirm what I already know in my hearts to be truth."

Noralla smiles. "I will pray to the gods for your success, Brother."

She turns to leave, but I call out, stopping her. "Noralla?"

"Yes?"

"Thank you, dear sister."

She beams. "I wish you nothing but happiness, Llyr."

"And what of your own?" I ask, remembering her broken betrothal to Varus. She did not love him, but I've often wondered if she feels hurt because she was rejected for another. If she does, she has mentioned nothing—then again, I have never asked.

"I am content for now. No one has caught my attention. Yet," she adds with a faint smile.

My mother walks out onto the balcony and we turn to face her. A faint grin tugs at her lips. "I thought I might find you both here."

Her gaze shifts to me. "Are you still thinking of the human?"

I sigh heavily in frustration. "Her name is Talia, Mother. And she is my linaya."

Mother lowers her gaze. "I have heard they are fragile creatures compared to our kind. Are you certain you wish to be bonded to her?"

"Yes," I reply without hesitation. "If she accepts me, I will take her as my mate."

"Sorella is still interested in you," she offers.

I shake my head. "Sorella is only interested in my title. Not me."

Mother's eyes drop to my chest, and she gives me a pitying gaze. "What if she still refuses to accept you without the mark?"

Before I can answer, Noralla steps forward, arching a brow. "Did not the same thing happen between you and father?"

Having overheard our conversation, Father's deep voice answers from the doorway. "Your mother refused to believe me, at first, when I told her that we were fated. The mark did not appear on my chest for several months." He moves to her side and brushes her long blue hair back from her face, tucking it behind her ear as he smiles. "You were a stubborn one, weren't you, my beloved?"

Mother laughs softly. "Yes, but eventually you won me over, did you not?"

Father turns to me. "It sounds like your female is stubborn as well. So, you will have to try harder to woo her."

I arch a brow. "You approve of me taking a human mate?"

Father places a hand on my shoulder and meets my eyes evenly. "I just want you to be happy, my son."

Mother huffs out a frustrated sigh. "Do not encourage him. You have yet to even meet her. You should wait until you have seen the humans before you condone—"

"Condone what?" my father frowns. "If your parents had their way, you and I would not be together. Or have you forgotten how they were against our match in the beginning?"

She crosses her arms over her chest. "Of course, I have not forgotten."

He looks between me and Noralla. "And now we have these two perfect children that would never have been here if your family had had anything to say about it."

"Fine," Mother concedes. "You are right." She looks to me. "I have always wanted you to find a worthy mate. I just worry that this human female is not strong. I have heard their species are defenseless." She wrings her hands. "How would she protect your fledglings if you had any?"

My personal guard, Arnav, steps forward. His purple scales blend into the shadows so easily, I'd almost forgotten he was still nearby. His blue eyes look to my mother. "The human females may be small but they are strong in other ways, my queen."

A smirk twists my lips for I know he is just as captivated with one of the human females as I am with Talia. He has not admitted this to me, but I know it is truth. I saw the despair in his eyes as he said goodbye to Maya when we left the Fire Clan territory, and I remember the hope that sparked deep within them when he learned the humans would be coming here soon.

Arnav is our most trusted guard; respected by all. Mother

purses her lips a moment before her expression softens. "All right. I will withhold my judgement until after I meet her."

I smile.

Noralla steps forward and takes our mother's hands. "You'll like her, Mother. I'm certain of it."

CHAPTER 13

TALIA

As we fly toward the Water Clan territory, I force myself to focus on the ground below. I observe the desert plains give way to green fields and hills lush with vegetation. It's such a strange and striking contrast to the Fire Clan lands, making me long to explore more of this world.

The air grows cooler, and I peer ahead, my mouth drifting open in wonder at a vast blue ocean. We make a wide arc over the sea, and I smile as I watch a school of fish racing beneath the water. Giant waves crash against the cliff wall below an enormous castle. White towers proudly reach toward the blue sky. The silver-capped domes gleam beneath the sun, reminiscent of the Fire Clan castle.

The Capital City, Elaris, seems to be made up of several islands amidst the vast ocean. They are closely bunched together. White buildings, made of the same beautiful stone as the castle, dot the landscape. It reminds me a bit of ancient Greek structures that used to be on Earth.

I note, however, that humans would never be able to get from one to another without the help of a Drakarian. Bridges would definitely be a "must have" in this place if any of us were to settle here.

I shake my head softly. Why am I even thinking about this? It's not as if I'm going to move to the Water Clan territory. My thoughts drift to Llyr. I'm anxious to see him but worried as well. It hasn't been that long since he left, but it feels like an eternity to me.

Part of me worries that he may have forgotten me and moved on. He is a prince after all, and I'm sure there is no shortage of females ready to vie for his hand. I've purposely avoided asking Varus any questions or if he has heard anything in regard to this, because if Llyr has moved on, I'll be devastated.

We land in the center of a courtyard overgrown with vivid flowering plants. Gorgeous blooms of blue, purple and yellow fill the entire space. Long vines trail down and over the garden walls, swaying gently in the salted breeze like living curtains.

Rakan touches down so lightly I don't even know we've landed until he wraps his tail around my waist to gently lower me to the ground. I turn to thank him but trail off in awe as the dragons transform back into humanoid form. It's so incredible, I'm not sure I'll ever get used to seeing that.

As I turn my gaze back to the castle, hope flares inside me anew. I send a silent prayer to whomever may be listening that when I see Llyr this time, his chest will have the glowing fate mark pattern on his scales, telling me that he is mine. I've missed him so much.

CHAPTER 14

LLYR

Time has crept by, but the day of the celebration has finally arrived, and I am eager to see my linaya. The humans wanted a dance—a ball, they called it—to mark the celebration. Balls are an old Earth tradition, apparently. As I stand on the balcony overlooking the large, open room, I scan the crowd for Talia. I chose this vantage point specifically so that I could locate her the moment she arrives.

Below me, floor to ceiling windows line the far wall. We chose this space because it has a gorgeous view of the deep blue ocean. A floating chandelier above casts a soft glow throughout the entire space, highlighting the intricate tile inlay on the floor, depicting great swirling images of the sea.

Everything is open and airy and the crisp saline breeze drifts up from the ocean below. Noralla oversaw the decorations, choosing intricately carved tables, chairs and furnishings that have not been used since the last great peace gathering here many cycles ago.

A long table off to the side is overflowing with food and

drinks. Tall, fluted crystal glasses and silver trays of food are spread out in a beautiful display. I hope the humans are pleased with our efforts. More specifically, I hope that Talia enjoys it most of all. Perhaps she will be further enticed to accept me when she sees our castle decorated at its finest.

My hearts tap a frantic beat as I consider what I will tell her. I worry that she will reject me again, but I know I must try. She is mine. I am certain; I need only convince her. I am a patient male, and I will wait as long as she needs to accept me, for I know that I could never love another as I love her.

This great hall is typically reserved for Clan-wide feasts and banquets, but this day, a large space in the middle of the floor has been cleared so that the humans may dance. A beautiful melody played on stringed instruments drifts up from below.

Although we prefer to keep mostly to ourselves, my planet still deals with other races in the Galactic Federation Council. Through a vid feed connection, we obtained various samples of music for the humans to choose from. Varus and Raidyn said their mates were delighted when they listened to the selection.

I spot Lilliana dancing with her mate, their movements so synced that they practically glide across the floor, spinning and whirling in an intricate display of give and take. King Raidyn does the same with his mate Skye nearby.

Once again, jealousy batters at my chest as I think of Talia. I wish more than anything that she would agree to be mine.

The humans are clothed in elaborate robes they call dresses. In all my travels off-world, I have never seen designs such as these. The robes are so different from anything a Drakarian might wear. Varus said the tailors were excited to create a new style of clothing.

The females each wear floor-length, flowing dresses of

silkara that gather at the waist and flare at the hip. Intricate designs are stitched into the material. Each female has personalized her dress with unique colors and patterns. I find myself wondering what Talia chose to wear. My hearts pound in anticipation of finally seeing her again.

We have only found twenty human females, so it shouldn't be hard to spot Talia in the crowd below. However, I am disappointed when I do not find her.

Despair fills me at the thought that she may not have come. After all, Varus claimed he offered them the choice to stay in Fire territory if they did not wish to attend this celebration. Perhaps she decided to stay in the desert, after all, to avoid me after what happened between us the last time I saw her.

I'm so lost in my devastation that I don't notice Sorella approaching until she begins to speak. I notice she is wearing a dress similar to the humans' garments. The white fabric is a sharp contrast to her aqua-colored scales. She stares down at the humans with a look bordering on disgust. "They are pitiful creatures, are they not?"

My head jerks toward her. "No, they are not."

She gapes at me, then narrows her yellow eyes as if my words have angered her.

"They are survivors who left their dying world in search of a new life," I explain. "They couldn't know what they might find in the void, and yet, they took that chance. Can you think of anything more challenging and brave?" I arch a brow, waiting for her to answer. When she does not, I continue, "I admire their tenacity. They manage to thrive on a foreign planet."

"Really, Llyr," she admonishes, batting her lashes. "You give them far too much credit."

In truth, Sorella is an attractive female. She presented herself to me two cycles ago, offering herself as my mate. At the time, I suspected she was merely interested in my title. She suggested as much when she made the offer, assuring me that the Healers claimed she was fertile. She could give me an heir, and I could give her the status she so desperately craved.

Her family is well off, among the wealthiest in our Clan. She does not need the title; she simply desires it, I suppose. Then again, many females have approached me for the same reason, never bothering to hide their true intent.

When I refused her, she tried to seduce me into the mating chase. I did not give pursuit because I wanted her to understand I am not interested in a female whose only strength is her beauty. I want a partner who is my equal—a mate who desires me for my character, not what my status can offer her.

My parents are blessed with a loving bond. My mother could have mated any male she desired, but she chose my father simply because they fell in love. She did so even before his fated mark appeared for her on his chest. It did not matter to her that she was royalty while he could claim no special standing among our people. I want a life as rich as theirs, full of love and laughter.

I struggle to hide my annoyance at Sorella's attitude toward the humans, as well as her attempts to entice me. I give her a polite nod meant as a dismissal, but she does not take the hint. I scoot closer to the edge of the balcony. Although I've already looked for Talia, I feel compelled to try again. I cannot believe she would choose to stay behind in Fire Clan territory—not after telling me how much she longed to see the oceans of our world.

My breath catches in my throat as my eyes land on a familiar figure ascending the stairs. My hearts skip a beat when Talia's stunning blue eyes meet mine. I fight against the urge to rush forward and gather her into my arms.

My gaze travels over her form and I realize that my memory is not as sharp as I believed, for she is even more beautiful than I remember. Her brown hair cascades down her shoulders in long, silken waves. She is dressed in a long, light-blue gown that accentuates the rich blue color of her eyes. The delicate material sways gently around her ankles as she walks. The sunlight reflects off the glittering fabric, lending her an ethereal beauty.

"Oh," she says, startled to see me. "I didn't realize you were up here." Her gaze sweeps to Sorella then back to me. "I —I didn't mean to intrude."

She turns to leave, but I call out, "Talia, wait!"

Panic constricts my chest. I am desperate to keep her from walking away from me. As if she will somehow disappear and never return.

She stops and spins to face me.

"I didn't know anyone was up here," she admits.

"It is all right," I reassure her. "I have been waiting for you to arrive."

She glances at Sorella. "But you have company. I don't want to interrupt."

"You are not interrupting. This is Sorella." I turn to the Drakarian female. "Sorella, this is Talia. My—" I stop short of calling her my linaya, cursing myself for the near mistake. I cannot call her mine before she has even agreed to be my mate. "My friend," I finally offer, remembering how she introduced me to her friends before.

Sorella gives Talia a slight nod of acknowledgment, but I read the displeasure in her eyes. Female Drakarians are not friendly even to each other. Why would she act any differently toward a human female?

"Talia."

My sister's voice draws my attention as she walks up the stairs. She smiles warmly at my mate.

"Hi, Noralla."

"We are so pleased you are here," Noralla's eyes dart to me, "aren't we, Llyr?" She looks at Sorella. "I believe your parents are looking for you."

Sorella narrows her eyes but bows her head nonetheless. She probably suspects that my sister is trying to get rid of her. "Thank you, Noralla." She bows again and then leaves.

My sister excuses herself soon after, leaving Talia alone with me. I will have to thank Noralla later for her help. Sorella has been a constant annoyance since we returned from Fire Clan territory. I have made it very clear that I do not desire her as a mate, but she refuses to accept this.

I am glad to have this time alone to speak with Talia. I have missed her brilliant mind and the beautiful sound of her voice.

CHAPTER 15

LLYR

A crisp, saline breeze drifts up from the sea, and I notice Talia shiver slightly from the chill. Removing my robe, I gently drape the fabric around her shoulders.

Her luminous blue eyes scan my form. A pink bloom spreads across her cheeks and she lifts her gaze back to mine. "Thank you," she murmurs.

I remember she told me that human skin changes color when nervous or attracted to someone. Now that my dear sister shared her suspicion with me, I hope it is truth—that her face reddens because she finds my now nude body appealing, not discomforting. I pray she is still waiting for my chest to display the fated mark and has not given up hope. Even if the glowing pattern never appears, I will do everything I can to convince her to be mine before she leaves again. I cannot bear another day without her.

I tip my head to the side. "I apologize. If my nudity bothers you, I can retrieve another robe." I've often heard from Varus and Raidyn that humans only discard their clothing to bathe or to mate. They find it strange that my people rarely bother with coverings. That is why I have been mindful to remain dressed in her presence at all times prior to now.

Her cheeks flush an even deeper shade of red. "No, that's all right. You don't have to do that."

I arch a brow. "You are certain?" The last thing I want is to make her uncomfortable.

"Yes."

Her gaze drifts over my shoulder to the ocean beyond the balcony. A dazzling smile lights her face. "It's beautiful up here."

"It is," I agree, though I am only looking at her. She is the most beautiful female I have ever seen.

The waves break along the shoreline below as a gentle breeze ruffles her long, brown hair—the sun's rays highlighting the various rich earth tones. My fingers flex with the urge to run my hands through the silken strands.

I long to pull her into my arms and hold her close. As the light dances across her bare shoulders, I imagine brushing my lips over her petal-soft skin, trailing a line of kisses down the elegant column of her neck. I desire more than anything to bind her to me—to claim her as mine.

However, I dare not touch her. She has not agreed to be mine—yet.

"Is my territory how you imagined it?" I ask as her eyes sweep over the sea.

She shakes her head softly, whispering, "It's so much more."

"What do you mean?"

A wistful smile curves her lips. "When I lived on the colony ship, I used to dream about the world we'd one day settle on.

I'd lie in my bed and watch the stars blur past the window, imagining a planet just like this. My father and I shared the same vision; he loved the sea, as well." Tears gather in the corners of her eyes, but she blinks them back. "I've always been drawn to the ocean. Even as a child, I was fascinated by the images of Earth-that-was before it was ruined beyond saving."

"The oceans on Earth—they were once similar to Drakaria's?"

"Yes. It's so beautiful here."

"I am pleased that you like my territory."

Silence settles in the space between us. She turns to face me and opens her mouth as if to speak but quickly snaps her jaw shut when a servant appears.

It's difficult, but I somehow manage to suppress my irritation at his terrible timing as he offers us a tray with two plates of food, bowing gracefully. "A meal for you and your guest, my prince."

We follow him to a nearby table on the balcony and he places one plate in front of each of our seats.

"Thank you." I turn to Talia. "Are you hungry?"

"Starving."

My eyes fly wide. "Is there not enough food in the Fire Clan for your people?" I struggle to suppress the growl building in my chest at the thought that Varus may be unable to provide for the humans but too proud to admit it.

My concerns quickly disappear when she laughs. "Believe me, if anything, they give us too much food. Several of us have started gaining some unwanted weight."

She pats her stomach as if this were the case for her. In truth, I would rather she carry more weight. Her slim, delicate form worries me. I know her size is typical of her species, but it calls forth my protective instincts so strongly that I fear I will become an over-possessive mate, should she accept me. Drakarian females dislike this quality in a male, and I wonder if humans feel the same.

She stares at her plate. "The portions on this tray are a lot bigger, do you want to switch? I don't think I can possibly eat all of this."

The servant spins to face her. "This plate was prepared especially for you."

"Oh." She gives him a faint smile. "All right."

I am glad she does not choose to switch with me. I prefer my mate to be well fed.

"I've never seen this kind of food before."

Of course, she hasn't. "They are specific to Water Clan territory," I explain, pointing to the meat. "This is hareti and this," I point to the fruit, "is lanira."

I lift the hareti to my mouth, but before I can take a bite, I notice the slight grimace on her face. I put the meat down with a matching frown. "What is wrong?"

She hesitates. "It's just... I'm a vegetarian."

"What do you mean?"

"I prefer to eat only fruits and vegetables. No meat."

An image of her flat white teeth bared in a smile flits through my memory. Of course, she prefers to eat plants. She lacks the sharp fangs my people use to tear into meat.

I offer her my plate. "Would you like my fruit? I will take your hareti."

She smiles. "That would be great."

We trade and begin eating. I give her my fruit and then eat her larger portion of hareti since she does not want it. I push my plate aside, leaving my smaller portion for later. I am more interested in talking to her than eating. I have longed for her company and now that she is here, I will not waste this moment. I want to learn everything about her.

"Our cuisine includes many"—I pause, casting about for

the term she used—"vegetarian dishes. I will make certain the kitchen knows of your preference."

"Thank you, Llyr. That's really thoughtful of you."

"It is my pleasure."

As she studies me, I am completely mesmerized. She is beautiful, my mate, with dark hair that falls past her shoulders in gentle waves and petal-soft skin. Her deep blue eyes captivate me most; in their depths, I see a future with her by my side.

Determination grants me renewed energy. If I want a life with her, I must win her heart.

I notice she has finished eating, so I hold my hand out to her. "Would you like to see more of my territory?" If she falls in love with this land, perhaps she will choose to stay and give me more time to woo her.

She smiles as she takes my hand. "Yes, that would be wonderful."

I lift my gaze to the sky. The cloud cover is thin and the air is clear. These are perfect conditions to fly over the sea. "Do you trust me?"

Indecision plays out across her features. My hearts hammer, anxious and excited in equal measure to hear her answer. If she rejects me, I will be devastated. If she does not—

"Yes," she replies.

A brilliant smile lights my face. She trusts me. After all she has been through, this honor is more than I could have hoped for.

I step closer. "We are going to fly. Is that all right with you?" Although I have flown her before, I still ask, unwilling to pressure her.

Hesitation crosses her features. "I—I'm not—"

"I will remain in this form," I reassure her, knowing that my draka form may be the reason she is reluctant. After all, the last draka she flew with tried to steal her for the Wind Clan.

She nods. "All right."

Carefully, I place one arm behind her back and loop the other under her knees. I lift her into my arms and gather her close to my chest. She twines her arms around my neck, looking up expectantly. She fits so perfectly against me, as if she were made to be mine.

I spread my wings and note the awe on her face as she studies them. "Your wings. They're so beautiful."

Beautiful is not what a male wants to be called by his female, but I blame the translator chip. Perhaps it does not recognize her word for *handsome*. "Thank you," I reply.

We stand on the edge of the balcony. The deep blue ocean is stretched out before us. Light from the sun's rays scattered out across the water cast beautiful, shimmering reflections over the surface. Waves crash against the shoreline, sending a fine mist of spray up the cliff wall. The small droplets of moisture cling to Talia's hair as she looks up at me.

Her lovely smile makes my hearts stutter in my chest. How many times have I dreamed of holding her in my arms? Now that she is here, I must convince her to accept me as hers.

Leaving her was the most difficult thing I've ever done, and I do not wish to ever be parted from her again.

Extending my wings out fully, I catch the wind in my sails and step off the edge. A sharp yelp of surprise escapes her as we fall for a moment before we lift up into the current. She gives me a smile so dazzling it rivals the brightness of the Drakarian sun.

As we glide over the ocean, I swoop low. The water races beneath us and she extends her arm to dip one finger below the surface, gaping at our rippling reflection in wonder.

She laughs when a spray of foam hits us as a wave crashes

against a rock formation jutting above the surface. "This is amazing, Llyr!"

I circle in a long arc around the castle, wanting her to witness the beauty of our palace. If she decides to become my mate, this will be as much her home as it is mine. The prospect of presenting her to our people as my linaya and princess of the Water Clan floats to the surface of my thoughts. I have replayed this fantasy in my mind many times while we have been apart.

The castle sits on the edge of a cliff, which I regard with appreciation as we pass. My home is the most beautiful in all of the Clans. Massive waves break on the rock wall below. White towers reach for the sky, capped by silver, reflective domes. Several of my guards watch us fly by discreetly, their eyes tracking my mate with curious stares.

Fierce possessiveness moves through me. I struggle to suppress the growl that rumbles my chest. I dislike the idea of other males staring at my linaya.

"Can you fly back over the water?" she asks, and I turn to obey without hesitation. The farther we go from other males, the better, as far as I am concerned. I want her attention all to myself.

I race out to the sea, delighting in the joy brightening her features as we fly over the water. My hearts and mind feel lighter than they have in days. Euphoria overtakes me and I am so enthralled that I do not realize we have lost sight of the castle until I notice the wind picking up.

When I finally turn back in the direction of the palace, alarm bursts through me. Dark clouds gather on the horizon, heading to block our path. How could I have been so careless? Storms like these can approach without warning on the open sea.

"What is it?" she asks, sensing my panic.

"A storm. Moving fast," I explain. "We must find shelter now."

Fear wraps tight around my spine as I turn, searching for my home, but clouds block my view. I realize returning to the castle is no longer an option. Tempests out on the open ocean can be violent. If I were alone, I might be able to reach home, but I cannot risk flying my mate through a storm. She could be ripped from my arms, especially with the wind as strong as it is now.

Desperate, I scan for any place to land and take shelter. A thin line of green and purple in the distance catches my attention. I turn and race toward land, noticing that my wings feel sluggish and my movements uncoordinated.

A strange sensation suffuses my body and I suddenly feel as if I'm floating on a wave. I do not understand its cause, nor why my mind feels blanketed by a thick fog. I shake my head in an attempt to clear my thoughts.

"Are you all right?"

Though I don't want to instill panic in Talia, I also do not wish to hide the truth either. "I am uncertain." Blue eyes meet mine in concern. "Do not worry. I have enough strength yet to bring us to safety."

I had not wished to lie to her, but I have. I am not entirely sure I am strong enough to reach the island, but now that I have reassured her that I can, I vow to make the journey no matter what. I will not fail my mate.

I beat my wings furiously as we approach land. The gusting wind tries to rip my linaya from my arms, but I hold her tightly to my chest. She is more precious to me than anything in the world, and I will die before I let her go.

My mind feels as if it's shrouded in a thick fog as I struggle to search for somewhere to set down. My body is clumsy and uncoordinated, so I do not trust myself to touch down anywhere but the beach. The sand is soft and will cushion our landing.

As gently as I can, I set down. The moment my feet touch the ground, I collapse. I struggle to lift my head, and the world tilts and spins all around me. Using the last of my strength, I reach up to cup Talia's face. "Leave me, linaya. You must find shelter."

"Llyr, what's wrong?" she demands, panic lacing her tone.

"I—I do not know. But I cannot walk. You must leave me. Hurry."

"No, I won't leave you." She stares down at me, her eyes bright with tears. "I won't."

I open my mouth to argue, but my head lolls back and I fade away into the darkness.

CHAPTER 16

TALIA

I watch in horror as Llyr slumps onto the sand. "Llyr!" I cry. "Wake up!"

A cold wind whips around me, tearing at my form. Dark-gray clouds roll overhead, blocking the sunlight. Lightning streaks across the sky, followed by a deafening boom of thunder. Enormous waves rush toward the island, crashing violently on the shore.

The water gathers around us with each wave, threatening to pull us out to sea each time they retreat back into the ocean. I stare stubbornly at Llyr's prone form. He told me to go, but I refuse. If I leave him here, he'll drown.

Panic claws at my chest. I lean down to grab his forearm and pull with all my might. But it's no use—he's too heavy. Drakarians weigh two to three times more than a human. I grit my teeth in frustration when I realize he's barely budged. This isn't going to work.

Several scenarios play out in my mind, none of them ending well. I can't move him, I can't leave him, and I can't think of another solution. The ice-cold water is rising at an alarming rate. I lift his head into my lap to keep his face above water.

We don't have much time. *I'm an engineer*, I think, exasperated. *How can I not have a plan?*

A fresh wave pools around us, chilling me to the bone. Desperately, I gather my robe around my chest as if the water-logged material can somehow warm me.

I look down at the completely soaked fabric. The robe could help. A smile ghosts across my lips as I formulate a plan.

We're going to survive.

Rain pelts the earth in heavy sheets, turning the sand into a thick layer of mud. I quickly remove my robe and kneel beside Llyr. I roll the fabric up lengthwise, lay it along his form, and do my best to push as much beneath him as I can. I hurry to his other side and pull the fabric completely under his body, then tie the sleeves around his shoulders.

Moving to his head, I grab the hood of the robe and begin to pull. He's still heavy, but my makeshift sling works. The fabric glides over the mud as I drag him across the sand, one step at a time. My muscles ache in protest while I climb the steep slope away from the beach, but I refuse to give up. We're not going to die here—not today.

I keep my head down, forcing my feet to keep moving forward. Each step is agonizing, but we're making progress, and that's all that matters. As soon as we're far enough away from the tide that I do not have to worry about him drowning, I raise my hand to my brow, shielding my eyes from the rain to scan the area for anything we can use as shelter.

My parents spent hours in the virtual reality rooms, teaching me and my brother about survival in the wild. We hated the lessons at first, but they insisted we needed to learn so that we could thrive on our new planet. Eventually, we learned to love those outings with our family. I realize now just how wise my parents were to teach us these skills.

Shelter, water, food. My father told us that these were most important above everything else. I don't know what's wrong with Llyr, but I just need to find shelter right now.

One thing at a time, my father used to say. I repeat this mantra in my mind as I trudge up the beach. Up ahead, I notice a rocky overhang on a cliffside. It doesn't seem far, but I know looks can be deceiving.

"Difficult, but not impossible," I mumble to myself as I turn and start dragging Llyr toward the cover.

My arm and leg muscles burn, but I refuse to stop. Llyr is counting on me to save him. An image of my parents flashes in my mind. No, I will not leave him like I left them. Never again will I abandon someone I love. I no longer care that Llyr's chest doesn't display the fate mark for me—I love him, and that's all that matters.

Eternity seems to pass before I finally reach the rocky overhang, delirious with exhaustion. The entire island seems to be made up of rather mountainous terrain and covered in thick, purple and green foliage. If I'd visited the location on a pleasant day, I'd probably find this place beautiful—the perfect getaway spot for a couple on some sort of romantic vacation.

The rock overhang curves above our heads in a horseshoe shape. A waterfall spills down the center, from the mountain above, into a small pool below. If the water is fresh, like I suspect, then we have a drinking source. Now, I just need to worry about food.

The ground around the pool is high enough under the overhang that I don't think we'll have to worry about flooding, especially since the water drains off into a river that runs away from our new shelter and disappears into the thick vegetation of the jungle beyond.

Now that we're somewhat shielded from the storm, I can better appreciate our surroundings. Aside from the purple-colored vegetation, I could almost imagine we were on Earth.

But because I'm unfamiliar with this place, I need to take precautions. Worried that large predators could potentially prowl this island, I pull Llyr behind a boulder to hide us from unwanted eyes.

Panic rises as I study his limp form, but I push it back down. I need to focus. What I wouldn't give to wield the Earth Clan's healing fire right about now. I have no idea what's wrong with him. I trail my hands down his body to inspect him for injuries but find none. I don't understand how he could be fine one moment and collapse the next. It all happened so fast.

His breathing is soft and even, not labored—that must be a good sign. However, all the unknowns are battering at my sanity.

I can't contact his Clan for help. Even if I could, I have no idea how far the castle is. I wouldn't even be able to give the rescue party directions to this island.

I reach down and cup Llyr's face, turning him toward me as I brush my thumb lightly across his cheek. "Wake up, Llyr. I need you to open your eyes for me. Tell me what to do. What do you need, my love?"

My love. The words escape my lips unfiltered. It's true—I love him, no matter how often I've tried to convince myself that I shouldn't.

My stomach twists as a terrible thought creeps in. He may never open his eyes. He may never wake up. He could die and leave me stranded here.

I swallow the lump in my throat and lift my gaze to the jungle bordering our shelter. I understand enough about nature that I could probably survive out here, but I don't want to be alone. I don't want to lose Llyr.

I ignore my rumbling stomach. Night is falling and I'm hesitant to leave Llyr in search of food. At least we have a reliable water supply. I can hold off on tending to my needs a bit longer; right now, my main concern is him.

I draw in a deep breath, shuddering. My clothes are thoroughly soaked. The last thing I need is to catch a cold, so I peel off my clothing, including my bra and underwear. Everything needs to dry. Draping my dress and undergarments on a nearby rock, I pull the robe from under Llyr and shake it out to dry as well.

He shivers, so I touch his forehead, finding his skin hot to the touch. I have no idea what a Drakarian's normal body temperature might be; I hardly touched him before today. So, I do the only thing I can: I curl up beside him, nestling as close to his chest as I can in hopes that the warmth of my body will somehow help him.

His proximity is definitely helping me. As if to emphasize that thought, a cool breeze whips through the shelter. I instinctively bury my head in Llyr's chest. He moans lightly, and I lift my hand to stroke his cheek. "Llyr, I found shelter. We're safe for now, my love. You just rest and recover, all right? I'll take care of you."

My voice must reach him even while unconscious because he settles and his breaths even out again. The gentle rise and fall of his chest and the beat of his hearts against mine comforts me. He's still alive.

I close my eyes and try to sleep, but the storm raging outside thwarts my efforts. My thoughts turn to my parents again and I replay the nights they took Milo and me camping in the virtual reality room. Even though my mother and father claimed they were teaching us survival skills, I know they enjoyed those mini-vacations as much as we did.

This time is different, however. My actions will have real consequences. The camping excursions on the ship never included any true element of danger—that's part of the reason they were so fun. I wonder how well those survival skills will serve me on Drakaria.

I sigh heavily in frustration. The Drakarians aren't primitive by any means. They have tech we humans never even dreamed of, including their incredible translators. I should have spent some time familiarizing myself with it all and reading up on this world.

Instead, I've been so preoccupied with planning the construction of lifts and bridges in the Fire Clan capital that the thought never crossed my mind. All I've been studying is the desert terrain and Drakarian methods of engineering.

I know I can lie here all night and mull over what I should have done, but my time is better spent getting some rest and starting the search for food early in the morning. Although I hate the thought, fish must swim in these waters, and it's safer to catch one than to risk my life consuming the purple berries I spotted on a few of the bushes we passed.

I refuse to believe that Llyr won't wake up. He has to.

When he does, he'll need food and water, and I plan to provide him with both.

I'm worried about potential predators, but I'm so exhausted I can barely keep my eyes open. Unable to fight back my fatigue, I close my eyes and send a silent prayer to whoever may be listening that nothing bothers us. I drift away into the darkness of sleep.

CHAPTER 17

TALIA

When I open my eyes, I'm not sure how much time has passed. Llyr is still unconscious. The worst of the storm seems to have moved on. Thick gray clouds cover the sky, blocking most of the light from the sun, but at least I'm able to see.

Our limbs tangled while we slept and something hard presses against my abdomen. Although I've never seen one, I suspect what I'm feeling is Llyr's *stav*—as the Drakarians call their manhood.

Carefully, I inch away from him, but his arms tighten around me and he breathes my name like a sigh.

"Llyr?" I whisper. "Are you awake?"

His eyes remain closed and he only responds, "Mine."

A growl rumbles his chest as he nuzzles my hair.

I'm glad he's awake enough to move, but I wish he were fully conscious. I love the feel of his strong body wrapped around mine, and would gladly stay like this, but I need to get moving. I wait a moment for him to relax his hold on my body then quietly slip from his grasp.

My bra and underwear are dry, though my dress and robe are still damp. I know nudity is no big deal to Drakarians, but I need to look out for our survival, and I dislike the idea of running around on the island naked.

I dress in my bra and underwear then kneel beside Llyr. Gently, I cup his cheek and turn his face to mine. "I'll be back as soon as I can, all right? I'm going to find you something to eat."

His brow furrows softly as if he heard me but didn't understand. I smile, leaning down to press a quick kiss to his forehead before I head out to check if these waters have fish. I suspect they do, but I'm not taking anything for granted.

As I step from our shelter, I scan my surroundings. The storm has left the island a mess. Several trees are downed, with branches and debris scattered everywhere. Blocking out the destruction, I force myself to focus. My father once told me anyone can survive in the wilderness as long as you keep your wits about you.

Something moves in the sand ahead. I freeze when I realize several somethings are moving. Cautiously, I approach, releasing a sigh of relief when I find fish flopping in the surf.

At least, that's what they resemble. These fish are bigger and more vibrant colored than anything I ever saw in images of Earth. They must have washed up with the storm's waves and been stranded along the beach.

I need some way to carry them all, so I rush back to the overhang and grab the robe. It doesn't take long to gather a dozen fish, tie them up in the material, and bring them back to our shelter.

Now, I just need to figure out how to start a fire. Even if Llyr were awake, I don't think he could help me. According to Lilly, only some Drakarians can breathe flame; the Water Clan spits frostfire, which doesn't burn hot.

Unfortunately, the branches that litter the ground are still wet. The small blaster in my thigh harness could heat something, but I have no tinder that will catch and stay lit.

Unless...

I gather several downed, broken limbs and arrange them in a pile. Once they dry, I can use a tuft of my hair as kindling. If I hit it with the highest setting on the blaster, I could start a fire.

I lay my cache of fish across several rocks. If worse comes to worst, I suppose I'll have to eat them raw. The very thought sickens me, but we don't have much choice. To survive, we will have to make do with the available resources.

In the meantime, I rip a long strip of fabric off my dress and carry it to the pool. I dip the material into the water and wring it out until it looks clean. The water smells fresh, and when I taste a drop, I don't notice any salty or bitter contamination. Since I have no better way to test the pool, I have to assume it's safe.

I dip the fabric into the water again and return to Llyr's side. I wring it gently over his lips, hoping he'll drink some. At first, he doesn't move, but after a moment, he opens his mouth to catch a few drops of liquid.

Encouraged, I lift his head into my lap and then give him the rest slowly because I don't want him to choke. His eyelids flutter, and I smile down at him. "Llyr, I'm here. You're safe. I'm taking care of you, but you need to wake up, my love. Please."

He reaches up and grasps my hand, giving me a weak yet reassuring squeeze.

"Do you want more water?" I ask.

He barely manages to nod, and I fetch more.

After he's finished drinking, he falls asleep again. I'm

disappointed that he can't stay awake for long but encouraged that he was conscious at all. That means he's improving.

"All right," I tell him. "I have a blaster, but I'm going to make us a spear. Two weapons are better than one."

His eyes remain closed and he doesn't respond, but that's okay. At least he was able to hydrate.

All I can do now is keep watch and wait for him to wake. The island has been relatively devoid of any noises aside from the dull roar of the sea, but that doesn't mean we're alone here. I have no idea what might make its home in this land and I need to be prepared to defend us from predators if need be.

Eyeing a long, straight branch, I start whittling one end with a sharp rock. After some trial and error, I finally get the right angle and carve the limb into a sharpened spear. I smile as I study my work. Now I have a spear for fishing and a sharp weapon to defend us with if I have any problems with the blaster.

I sit beside Llyr, propping my back against a boulder with my blaster in one hand, spear in the other. "I'll keep watch," I tell him. "You just focus on getting better."

He moans lightly, and hope fills me. Maybe he'll wake again soon.

CHAPTER 18

LLYR

My eyes snap open to unfamiliar surroundings. My head pounds as I turn to find Talia slouched against a boulder by my head, fast asleep. She grips a blaster in one hand and a long wooden spear in the other.

How long have I been asleep? Was she keeping watch over me?

I sit up and the world spins for a second before finally settling. I glance again at Talia, who is dressed only in her undergarments—as the humans call their little strips of clothing. I notice the rest of her clothes, including my robe, are laid across some rocks to dry.

Beside the fabric, several dead fish lie on the rocks. Did she gather food for us? I study her intently. Though she may appear small and fragile, she has the heart of a survivor, just as I suspected.

"Talia?" I call softly so as not to startle her.

Her eyes snap open. The moment she sees me, she rushes

115

forward, throwing her arms around my neck. She presses her lips to my face in a series of urgent kisses. I understand her actions only because I have observed Varus's mate do the same to him. My people do not customarily kiss.

"Thank the Stars you're awake." Her breath is warm in my ear as she wraps her arms around me, hugging me tightly.

"How long have I been unconscious?"

She lifts her gaze to the darkened sky. "To be honest, I don't know. The worst of the storm has passed, but I haven't seen the sun since we left your castle." She reaches up to cup my cheek, studying me with a concerned frown. "I don't understand what happened. You suddenly had trouble flying. You barely made it here before you collapsed."

The acute nature of my symptoms, along with the pounding headache and discomfort in my stomach, is consistent with vimar poisoning. If my tongue is bright red, I can be certain this is the case.

"Is my tongue red?" I ask Talia, opening my mouth wide.

She gives me an incredulous look but examines my tongue anyway. "Yes. Why?"

"I believe I ingested poison," I tell her. "All my symptoms fit."

"Poison?" Her brows shoot up toward her hairline.

I search my hazy memory. "All I ate before we left was your hareti meat," I tell her.

Anger churns in my gut as I remember how the servant insisted that she take the plate he offered her when she expressed a desire to switch with me.

She must have reached the same conclusion as I have because she scowls. "If that's all you had, then that means someone wanted to poison me. Remember the server?"

I give her a grim nod.

"But who would want to do that? Why me?"

116

My jaw clenches. "I believe I know who tried to hurt you—Sorella. The female I introduced you to on the balcony."

"Why?"

"She desires to be my mate, but she knows that I only want you."

A pink flush blooms across Talia's cheeks and the bridge of her nose at my words. She seems hesitant. "But, Llyr, I—"

I reach for her hand. I've held her hand before, so I'm surprised at the suddenly rough texture of her skin. Turning her palm up to my gaze, I inhale sharply when I see blisters have begun to form on the delicate flesh. I start to ask where these came from, but then my eyes find her spear's sharpened point.

She pulls her hand from mine, rubbing the skin gently. "It's fine. Really," she says. "It's just a few blisters."

I'm ashamed of my inability to protect her. Memories of collapsing on the beach during the storm flood my mind. "How did we get here?" I lift my gaze to the rocky ledge that hangs above our heads. It provides adequate shelter and water trickles down the rocks nearby. "Did you carry me?"

That seems unlikely, given that I weigh two or three times more than her.

She lifts her shoulders, then drops them. "Sort of."

My mouth hangs open. "But how?"

She proceeds to tell me about how she used the robe to drag me. I do not know how far she moved my unconscious form from the beach, but any distance would be a feat. I am amazed by her ingenuity as well as her strength.

"Do you know this island?" she asks. "Where we are in relation to the castle?"

Grinding my teeth in frustration, I shake my head. "Forgive me. The poison clouded my mind and I—"

"*Shhh.*" She places a finger to my lips to silence me. "You don't have to apologize." She cups my cheek again with her hand, her blue eyes piercing mine. "I'm just so glad you're awake." She gestures to the fish. "I gathered those from the beach. Are you able to eat?"

I shake my head again. "My stomach still aches. But I believe I will drink some water."

I stand, meaning to walk toward the waterfall, but I stumble over my own feet. She wraps an arm around my torso to help me.

I steady myself using her as my anchor, but I know she cannot support my weight. So I simply thank her and allow her to guide me to the small pool beneath the rocky ledge. I do not hesitate to cup my hands and drink the crystal-clear, refreshing water.

I turn to her. "What about you? Are you hungry? Thirsty?"

"Both," she admits with a faint smile. "But I didn't know if those purple berries," she gestures to a nearby lomar plant, "were safe to eat."

My eyes widen. "They are poisonous."

"Good to know."

I send a silent prayer to the gods, thanking them for granting me such an intelligent mate. If she had not thought to wait, she could have ingested the berries and died before I ever awakened.

She turns her gaze to the fish. "Can you start a fire?"

With a heavy sigh, I shake my head. "No. I only possess the ability to breathe frostfire." As I scan our surroundings, I realize how worthless this ability is to us. Would that I could breathe flames instead, like the Fire Clan.

"No problem," she chirps, surprising me with her optimism. "My parents taught me all kinds of survival skills. I think I can get a fire going."

"How?"

She wraps her arm around me again, helping me back to

our small nesting area. Only now do I notice she has piled several branches and twigs beneath the overhang.

She grins. "Watch and learn."

I observe, growing more distressed by the second, as she plucks several long, silken hairs from her scalp, wincing slightly. I shake my head emphatically. "If you need hair, you should take mine. I do not want you to hurt yourself."

"You're so thoughtful, Llyr. But I'm all right. Besides, you're still recovering."

Her words return my attention to the poison. As small as she is, the dose of vimar I ingested would likely have been lethal to her. I shudder inwardly before anger boils in my gut. When we reach the palace, I will question Sorella. If she is guilty as I suspect, she will pay for daring to try to harm my mate. *My vow.*

"Stand back," Talia warns, her gentle voice pulling me back from my dark thoughts.

I watch as she aims her blaster at the small pile of wood, noting the strands of dark hair on top. A smile curves my lips. She uses her hair as kindling. My mate is very clever.

She fires the blaster, and I watch the hair burst into flame, catching the wood below on fire. She turns to me triumphantly. "Ta-da!"

"Ta... da?"

"It's an expression. It means you should be impressed by my survival skills." She grins.

I return her smile. "Ta-da!"

She barks a laugh, and it is the most beautiful sound I've ever heard. I stand in awe of her beauty and brilliance. "Where did you learn how to do this?"

"My dad taught me how to make fire." She lifts and drops her shoulders again. "He was trying to prepare us for settling on a brand-new world."

"He was a wise man, your father."

119

She lowers her gaze to her hands. "He was," she agrees. "So was my mom. I'm holding on to the hope that somehow, my parents made it to one of the other escape pods. Milo is certain they're dead, but I..." She draws in a deep breath. "I feel in my heart that they're alive somewhere... somehow. I can't explain it. I just can't believe that they're truly gone. When we were evacuating the ship, everything happened so fast. I wanted to look for my parents, but there wasn't time and—" Her voice catches.

A tear escapes her lashes and rolls down her cheek. I reach out and brush it away with the pad of my thumb then pull her to my chest. She sobs against me and the sound of it breaks my hearts.

Gently, I run my hand over her hair and down her back in a soothing gesture. I wish I could take this terrible pain away from her, but I cannot. I can only offer what my people have already pledged. "We are still searching for more escape pods from your ship, Talia. Each of the four Clans has joined in this cause."

"Thank you," she whispers.

"We have several ships scouring this quadrant of space, in case not all of the pods made it to Drakaria. And we've contacted other races and asked for their aid in finding your people as well."

She blinks up at me. "You have? I didn't know that."

I nod. "We are part of the Galactic Federation of Planets. We have many allies. And although we prefer to keep to ourselves, many Drakarians still travel the stars. We have contacted them, and they have agreed to search for your kind."

A stunning smile curves her lips, making me glad to have shared this news. I send a silent prayer to the gods that we find her parents and the rest of her people soon.

I watch as she picks up a twig from the ground and uses it

to skewer two of the fish. She sits and holds the small branch over the fire. "You can have the first two fish while I cook the rest."

She is a survivor, my linaya. I smile brightly. "You are as intelligent as you are beautiful, Talia."

Her expression falls, and I realize I've said the wrong thing.

"Forgive me, I—"

She shakes her head softly. "No, Llyr. I should be the one apologizing to you. I hated how I left things between us before you returned home."

"Does this mean you've reconsidered becoming my mate?"

She lowers her eyes. "I—I do have feelings for you, Llyr. But"—her gaze drifts to my chest, searching futilely for the fate mark that, to my distress, still refuses to appear—"I thought I could… but I can't risk my heart knowing that you might be meant for someone else."

I reach out and stroke her cheek. Leaning in, I gently press my forehead to hers. Staring deep into her lovely blue eyes, I give her my truth. "I only want you, Talia. No one else. Even if the fate mark appeared for someone else, it would not matter. You are the female who has captured my hearts. My vow."

Her gaze holds mine for a moment before she gently presses her lips to mine and my mind stops functioning.

Her lips are warm and softer than I imagined. Her tongue darts out to trace the seam of my mouth as if asking for entrance. When I open to her, her tongue finds mine and curls around it.

Her taste is exquisite. I love the way her smooth tongue moves against mine, exploring my mouth. Varus told me about kissing and, if that is what this is, I want more. I cup the back of her neck and wrap my other arm around her waist, pulling her closer.

Her heart beats wildly in her chest against mine as I run my fingers through her long, silken hair. "You are perfect," I whisper against her lips. "Tell me you are mine, for I am already yours, my linaya."

She pulls back just enough to look up at me, and my hearts sink when I recognize the hesitance in her expression. "I'm sorry, Llyr. I—I shouldn't have done that."

I search her face in confusion. "Why? It was wonderful, my mate."

She gives me a pained look. "What if you're fated to love someone else?"

"Never," I deny vehemently. "You are mine, Talia. The fate mark will come—I know it will. And when it does, it will shine only for you."

She shakes her head as another tear slips down her cheek. "How do you know?"

I take her hand and pull it to my chest. "I feel it here. That is how."

"I just… I don't know," she finally mumbles, lowering her gaze. "I'm so afraid that I'll lose you to someone else."

I place two fingers under her chin to tip her head back up. "Know this," I murmur. "I will wait however long you need to decide you want me as much as I want you, Talia. I love you, and nothing will change that. I swear it to the stars."

She stares at me, eyes swimming with tears, but says nothing.

I stand. To prove to her that I will be a good mate, I must first take her back to safety.

"What are you doing?" she asks, her gaze traveling up and down my form in concern. "You're still not steady on your feet. You need to rest."

I shake my head. "No. I must get us back to the castle."

Cautiously, I emerge from beneath the ledge and search the night sky, hoping to find a star that will guide us back to the palace. I bite back a growl of frustration when I see that dark clouds block my view of the heavens. Although the worst of the storm has passed, the aftershocks are still brewing above. A loud crack of thunder fills the air, followed by a streak of lightning.

"What is it?" Talia asks.

"I cannot see the stars to guide us home," I lament. "The clouds are too thick."

She nods. "It's all right. Maybe tomorrow you'll be able to see the sky. For now," she gestures to the fish and the pool of water, "we have shelter, food, and something to drink. We'll be all right, Llyr."

I'm stunned by not only her words but the conviction behind them. A Drakarian female would be angry that I could not return her home immediately. She would threaten to sever our ties if we were already betrothed. If not, she certainly would never consider me a mate, much less touch me as Talia did earlier. In a Drakarian female's eyes, I would have already proven myself an unworthy failure.

She yawns and I return to her side. "You are tired. You should rest."

She does not hesitate to nod, which tells me she must be exhausted. I hate that she had to care for me and place my needs above hers while I was unconscious. I should be the one proving my worth to her.

She lies down behind the boulders where she created our nest. I quickly retrieve my robe from the rock and lay it on the ground as a blanket for her. She smiles up at me. "Thanks."

I return to our fire and add more wood so that it does not burn down to mere embers.

"Good idea," she mumbles sleepily. "The light might help keep predators away."

"Any predators nearby should be able to scent me," I tell her. "They will recognize me as the superior predator and should leave us alone."

A grin tugs at her lips. "I feel safer already."

I cannot tell if she speaks truth or jests, but I don't have much time to consider before I notice her shivering. I lie down beside her and wrap my arm around her waist, tugging her into my chest.

She opens her mouth—to protest, I suspect—but when I wrap my wings around her, she sags against me. A small sigh of contentment escapes her lips and I smile, pleased that I can provide her with warmth, at least.

"You're like a heater." She snuggles closer. "I love it."

All I need is for her to love me as much as she loves the warmth I emanate. As she nestles into my embrace, I realize all hope is not lost.

CHAPTER 19

TALIA

Thick smoke fills the hallways as panicked screams echo through the ship. Milo holds my hand in a vise-like grip, dragging me down the corridor toward the escape pods. "Wait! What about Mom and Dad?"

"That part of the ship is already sealed off. They're gone, Talia!"

"Wait!" I wail.

Frantic, my eyes snap open and I jerk upright. Llyr's face is a mask of concern. "Talia, what is wrong?"

I open my mouth to speak, but the words won't come. Tears sting my eyes and blur my vision as the horrible memories of the pirate attack on the ship surface in my mind.

He takes my hand, tugging me back down. "Talia, what is it? Tell me. Please."

A broken sob escapes me. "I left them, Llyr. I left them to die. It all happened so fast. I should have gone back to look for them."

"Who?"

"My parents," I whimper.

Llyr gathers me close, and I bury my face in his chest.

"It was not your fault," he whispers. "You cannot blame yourself."

"I shouldn't have left them, Llyr. I shouldn't have."

"You would have died if you had stayed. Or been captured. Your parents wouldn't have wanted that."

I know he's right, but I cannot shed the guilt and the pain. Great, hiccupping sobs wrack my body as he soothingly strokes his hand up and down my back. In my mind, I know I should pull away. I've always prided myself on my independence. But right now, all I want is to be held and comforted. Now that my nightmare has brought back the traumatic memories, I cannot hold back my tears.

I love that Llyr doesn't try to convince me to calm down. He just holds me as he whispers in my ear, "I have you, my *linaya*. I am here."

Llyr is a good man, and I love him. Why can't I just surrender to my emotions? I've never taken a risk in my entire life. I've always played it safe.

That's why I chose engineering: There is a sort of comfort in working with numbers and systems. Either my model works or it doesn't—simple as that. That's also why I resolved that I wouldn't risk falling for a Drakarian unless I knew for certain he was mine.

But then I met Llyr. The more time we spend together, the harder it becomes to ignore my feelings. I love him, and I'm so tired of fighting it. I wish I could surrender, but my doubt insists that I hold back.

After what feels like forever, I'm finally able to catch my breath. We lie side by side, wrapped in each other's arms. He folds his wings around me once more, pulling me impossibly closer, and I relish the touch of his skin against mine, reminding me that he loves me.

He gently brushes the last of my tears from my cheek, his expression speaking of devotion and care. I could so easily give my life to this man. But I've already lost my parents and I cannot bear the thought of losing another loved one. If he ended up bonding to another, it would destroy me.

Even so, I do not pull away—I can't. I love being held. "Thank you, Llyr," I whisper. "I haven't dreamed about my parents in at least a few days. I'm sorry if I startled you when I woke up."

"You do not need to apologize." His warm gaze travels over me like a gentle caress. "I understand. You miss them."

I blink back fresh tears. "In my dreams, I always go back for them. And in my nightmares, they are always dead. But I have to believe in my heart that they survived."

"There is no shame in continuing to hope, Talia. But you cannot allow the nightmares to consume your life and prevent you from doing what you must to survive, as well."

He's right. "Maybe that's why Milo has accepted that we will never see our parents again." I allow my thoughts to escape unfiltered. "I hated him for it, at first. Especially when he would chastise me for suggesting they might still be alive somewhere."

"We all do what we must to protect our hearts." He pauses. "We lost many during the Great Plague—my Clan was devastated. Yet I can only imagine how difficult it must be to grieve a loved one without ever knowing if they are truly dead."

"What happened during the plague? Lilliana told me that the sickness mostly affected women. But where did it come from?"

He shakes his head. "We believe contact with another race

spread the plague to our planet. That is why we are reluctant to travel the stars anymore and prefer to keep to ourselves. We lost so many females, and most of those who survived are barren."

"That's terrible," I whisper.

"It is also why this new alliance between the Clans is so important. Before your people landed in the desert, we realized that we would have to work together toward a path of reunification to avoid extinction. A long time ago, we used to live as one before our ancestors split into the four Clans."

"What happened?"

He sighs heavily. "Thousands of cycles ago, there were four brothers, each vying for their father's throne. They fought many battles before finally splitting into four different territories.

"Aros," he continues, "was the first leader of the Fire Clan. Of the four brothers, he was the most aggressive. He chose the desert plains as his territory, for he believed them to be the most defensible due to the vast, barren lands that provide visibility in all directions.

"Vaidan was the first leader of the Wind tribe. He was born on the Wind territory's floating islands and refused to give up his home, so he claimed them for his own.

"Taizja chose to lead the Earth Clan. He tried desperately to convince his brothers to reunite, to no avail. So the Earth Clan has remained neutral until this day. They have never taken sides in a battle between the Clans.

"My ancestor, Llurryn, founded the Water Clan. He chose the territory near the ocean, believing it superior to all other lands due to our high vantage point atop the cliffs and the vast sea that borders us."

I've never heard how the four Clans began, so his historical account fascinates me. I want to hear more about his planet, but I'm so tired that my eyelids begin to droop.

Llyr gently nuzzles my temple. "Rest," he whispers. "I have you. Nothing will bother us here."

I nod and allow myself to drift away, wrapped in his arms and wings.

CHAPTER 20

TALIA

When morning comes, I wake still enveloped in Llyr's embrace. His larger form is curled protectively around me. I snuggle back into his chest, enjoying the feel of his warm body pressed against mine. I reach out to gently trace my fingers along one of the soft, leathery folds of his wing. It's a darker shade than his scales, a deep gray blue.

He nuzzles the back of my head, and I realize he's awake. "Do my wings bother you?" he asks, his voice rough with sleep. "I will move them if you wish."

"No, they don't bother me," I reply quickly, not ready to leave the comfort of his embrace just yet. "They're beautiful, Llyr. The oceans on Earth were various shades of blue and green. Your wings remind me of the waters of the Northern Sea." I turn in his arms to face him. "Whereas your scales"—I brush the tips of my fingers across the silken scales of his chest—"remind me of the Pacific Ocean."

"Is this a good thing?"

I nod as I allow my gaze to travel over his aristocratic face and the proud spiraling horns that sweep from his head, their ice-blue color reminding me of glaciers.

He watches me with such intense longing that my heart clenches. I love this man, but I cannot give him my heart. He insists that we're fated, but without the mark, I can't be sure.

With a heavy sigh, I sit up, immediately missing the touch of his arms and wings. My hair and skin are gritty with sand. "I think I'll go to the beach to wash off. I'll be back in a second."

It's an excuse, but I don't trust my ability to resist him any longer. I move to stand, but his large hand grips my forearm, stopping me abruptly. "Wait. It could be dangerous. I will go with you."

Part of me wants to argue that I can handle myself, but another realizes it would be foolish to refuse the company. After all, there's still so much I don't know about his world. "All right."

When we reach the beach, I'm still wearing only my bra and underwear. I would feel self-conscious, but we're alone and he's walking around with no clothes himself. I'm not as comfortable with nudity as he is, though. So I wade into the water without stripping entirely.

Llyr stays on the beach, scanning the gray sky and the dark clouds above.

"Do you think it will clear up by this evening?"

His frown answers for him, though he shakes his head.

"Maybe tomorrow, then?"

"Perhaps."

To be entirely honest, I won't be all that disappointed if we can't leave tonight. I loved sleeping in his arms and waking up wrapped in his wings. And yet, I realize just how dangerous this is. I'm losing my heart to this man when it could shatter into a million pieces someday. Why couldn't we be like Lilly and Varus or Skye and Raidyn? Both Drakarian mates displayed the fate mark right away, leaving no question that they were meant to be together.

I turn my attention back to the ocean. Although the water is relatively clear, I'm reluctant to venture too far because I don't know what creatures make their home beneath the waves. So I stay in the shallows, enjoying the feel of the warm water as I float on my back and stare up at the sky.

I've never swum in an ocean before. The closest I've ever come was on the virtual reality deck of the ship. I'm surprised by how authentic the program was, but nothing beats the actual experience.

Closing my eyes, I lie back and lazily float on the waves. I lift my head to make sure I'm not drifting too far from the shore. Llyr stands on the beach, his gaze scanning the ocean as if searching for any sign of danger.

The water is only knee-deep below me, so I'm not worried. Besides, if there were any danger in the shallows, I'm certain Llyr would have insisted I come back.

Something thick and slimy wraps around my leg. Thinking it's some sort of floating debris, I brush my hand over my skin to get rid of it.

Alarm bursts through me as it tightens around my thigh. I jerk up, and my eyes go wide when I realize it's a blue tentacle.

"Llyr!" My terrified cry is cut off as I'm dragged beneath the surface. My arms and legs flail wildly as I struggle to break free, causing the creature's grip to tighten even more.

Another tentacle twines around my arm and a third curls around my waist, pulling me deeper under the water.

I claw at each tentacle with my nails, to no avail. A huge bulbous head with beady yellow eyes and a gaping maw full of razor-sharp teeth rises from below. I scream and a stream of bubbles escapes my mouth, along with the last of my oxygen.

A disturbance in the water above me draws my attention, and I look up to see Llyr dive into the ocean in his *draka* form. He opens his mouth and I watch, stunned, as he sends a line of frostfire at the creature's head. The water turns to ice, encasing the monster.

He extends his claws and shreds the tentacles from around my body. Gathering me in his talons, he races back to the surface. My heart is pounding as we break through. I'm coughing and sputtering, my lungs burning for air.

He carefully lowers me onto the sand. Shifting back into his humanoid form, he lifts me into his arms and rushes to our shelter.

Gently, he lays me on the robe spread on the ground. He starts to move away, but I'm so shaken that I wrap my arms tightly around his neck, refusing to let him leave. A broken sob escapes my lips as tears stream down my face.

I could have died. That monster would have eaten me if he hadn't saved me.

"What was that thing?" I gasp, my entire body trembling with the echoes of remembered fear.

"A kragen," he replies. "They are usually only found in deep water. The storm must have driven it closer to shore."

He holds me, wrapping his wings tight around my form as I struggle to fight back my tears. "You are safe, Talia," he whispers in my ear. "You are safe, my *linaya.*"

Linaya. He calls me his fated one because he is confident that I am his.

His resolve breaks mine. Why am I fighting this? I love him. I could have died. I want to be with him, and I don't want to hold back anymore.

I pull away just enough to touch his cheek. His silver eyes search mine before I lean in and gently press my lips to his.

At first, he doesn't respond, but slowly, he moves his mouth against mine in a tender kiss that melts my heart. The kiss soon deepens when his tongue slips past my lips. The delicious ridges of his tongue stroke against mine, and I moan lightly into his mouth.

I'm not going to fight this anymore. I love him and I want him more than anything I've ever wanted before.

His strong hands grip my backside and pull me into his lap as he kisses me passionately, stealing the breath from my lungs.

"Mine," he growls against my lips. "Tell me you are mine."

"Yours," I agree in a breathless whisper.

Panting heavily, he studies me with a hungry gaze. "Are you certain?" he rasps. "You would be mine?"

All my doubt falls away as I meet his eyes evenly. I love this man. "Yes."

CHAPTER 21

LLYR

appiness brighter than a thousand stars fills my chest when she whispers, "Yes."

Unable to hold back my joy, I crush my lips to hers in a claiming kiss. I do not know how my people have lived for so long without kissing. It is the most exquisite pleasure and torture as I stroke my tongue into her mouth just as I long to stroke my stav deep in her channel and fully claim her as my mate.

The small band of fabric around her breasts rubs against my scales. I am desperate to feel her skin against mine with no barrier between us. She gasps when I slice away the fabric that hides her beauty from me. I long to touch her everywhere.

I trace my hand down her body, relishing the feel of her petal-soft skin beneath the tips of my fingers. She moans as I cup her breast, the soft mound so lush and giving beneath my palm.

Drakarian females do not have breasts like these; their

chests are hard and flat. I brush my thumb over the soft peak and it hardens into a bead beneath my hands, as if begging for my attention. She moans and arches against me, asking for more.

I have dreamed of touching her for so long. Now that I can, I want everything.

I press a series of kisses along her jaw and down the elegant curve of her neck, tasting the sweet salt of her skin. The scent of her arousal grows stronger, driving me mad with desire.

She guides my hand down to the juncture of her thighs. When I reach the small scrap of material covering her feminine place, I fist it in my hand. She inhales sharply when I rip it from her body. "You are mine," I tell her. "And I want nothing to hide your beauty from me."

She pulls back just enough to stare up at me, her pupils blown wide and her cheeks flushed with arousal. My stav lengthens and extends from my mating pouch, seeking the heat of her entrance. I am fully erect and painfully engorged. I long to sheathe myself deep inside her and claim her completely—mind, body, and soul.

Her lips part on a soft moan as my stav presses against her already slick folds. She reaches between us and wraps her hand around my length. I grit my teeth because her touch feels so good I am worried I may spill my seed before I enter her, and I do not want to waste it. I want every last drop of my essence to fill her womb.

"Llyr," she breathes against my lips. "I've never done this before. I don't know what to do."

I have heard her people do not always mate for life. And though I would not care if she'd had another mate before me, fierce possessiveness fills me at the knowledge that I will be the first and only male to touch her so intimately. "We will learn together, my linaya."

She pulls back and blinks. "You mean you've never—"

I shake my head. "My people mate for life."

She stares for a moment more, and I wonder if she hesitates because she doubts my skill as a lover without experience or if she is second-guessing the idea of becoming mine.

However, I am a determined male. I may be inexperienced, but I talked long into the night with Varus and Raidyn about pleasuring a human female.

"Talia, do you want me?" I ask because I must be sure.

She reaches up to touch my cheek as her blue eyes stare deep into mine. "Yes. I want you, Llyr."

I crush my lips to hers and then brush my thumb over the small bundle of nerves at the top of her folds. Talia reacts exactly as they explained; her entire body lights up with pleasure.

I smile against her lips. I must thank my friends later for sharing this information with me—perhaps I will even name two of our many future fledglings after them.

Talia digs her nails into my back, moaning loudly in my ear as I continue to tease at the softly hooded flesh between her thighs.

I press another series of kisses down her neck, traveling lower to her chest. She threads her fingers through my hair as I close my mouth over her breast, laving at the stiff peak with my tongue.

Her grip tightens and she rolls her hips against mine. A sharp hiss escapes me when my stav drags through her slick folds. I am desperate to enter her and claim her completely, but first, I want to give her pleasure.

I gently lay her back on the robe beneath us. Her long, brown hair spreads across the fabric like a beautiful halo as she watches me with a half-lidded gaze. She reaches up to pull my lips back down to hers, and I go willingly, bracing on my elbows so as not to crush her under my weight.

She opens her thighs and I settle my hips between them. "I want you, Llyr," she whispers. "Make love to me."

Her blue eyes pierce mine. I brush the damp hair back from her face. Cupping her cheek, I run my thumb lightly along her soft, pink lips as I stare down at her in wonder. "You are beautiful, my linaya."

A stunning smile crests her lips, momentarily stopping my hearts.

"Let me give you pleasure, my mate."

Nervously, she bites her lower lip and nods.

I move over her, pressing tender, open-mouthed kisses down the length of her form. Her entire body is so soft and giving, and I know I will never tire of touching her. I pause at the small dip in her abdomen. Humans do not lay eggs as Drakarians do. I know that someday she will carry our child in her womb. Fierce possessiveness overtakes me again at the mere thought, and my stav aches with the need to fill her.

I move lower and slide my hands between her thighs, carefully opening her to my gaze. The scent of her need is intoxicating. Her pink folds are glistening with sweet nectar that I long to taste on my tongue.

"May I taste you?" My voice is husky and deep even to my own ears.

Her lips are puffy and swollen with our kisses as she bends to meet my gaze. She nods and I dip my head between her thighs. The first swipe of my tongue through her folds is so exquisite that a growl forms in my throat. Her taste is even sweeter than I imagined, and I am hungry for more.

When I reach the small nub at the top of her folds, she arches against me and threads her fingers through my hair to hold me in place. I concentrate my attention on the sensitive flesh as I gently push the tip of one finger into her core. She is so small and tight. I worry that she will be unable to take my stav.

My linaya grips my horns, trying to take over and control her pleasure by rolling her hips against me. My name escapes her lips on a breathless moan as I insert another finger. "I want you, Llyr."

"I am yours, my beautiful mate," I whisper.

I band an arm over her hips to hold her in place as she writhes beneath my attentions. Her entire body goes taut for a moment, then she cries out my name as she floods my tongue with the sweet nectar of her release.

Panting heavily, she collapses back onto the robe. I press a soft kiss to the inside of her thigh then lift my head. She tugs at my shoulders, guiding me back up the length of her body until my face is even with hers. I kiss her lazily. When I pull back, she cups my cheek in wonder. "That was... there are no words," she breathes.

She traces her delicate fingers across my chest and I look down, hoping to see the swirling glow of the fate mark across my scales. Still, there is nothing, and I worry she will change her mind about us. I don't want to ask, but I must. "Do you still wish to be with me?"

Her blue eyes snap up to meet mine. "Yes," she whispers. "I'm just... so afraid to lose you, Llyr."

I shake my head softly. "You will never lose me, Talia."

A tear slips down her cheek and I quickly brush it away as I stare deep into her luminous gaze.

"I love you, Llyr. If you were human, there would be no mark to tell us if we're meant to be together. Instead, we would feel it here." She places her palm to my chest, between my hearts. "I was so afraid to let myself love you because I don't want to lose you to someone else." Her eyes brighten with tears. "I've lost so much, and I didn't think I could bear to lose any more. So I didn't want to risk my heart. If you were human, I would have allowed myself to fall for you from the beginning."

My hearts clench. "Do you wish I were human?"

"No." She presses a tender kiss to my lips. "I love you just as you are."

I cannot stop the grin that curves my mouth at her words. "You love me?"

"Yes," she murmurs, a tear slipping down her cheek. "And when I almost died today, I realized that I regretted not accepting you when I had the chance. So, I won't fight my feelings anymore. I don't care if you don't have the fate mark. If you tell me that you feel it here," she presses her palm to my chest once more, "and you tell me that you're mine, I believe you, my love. I want to be yours."

My hearts are full of wonder that this beautiful female would choose to be mine despite her fears and concerns. I am humbled beyond words.

"Tell me," she whispers as she brushes her thumb across my lower lip. "How does one bond to a Drakarian?"

A primal and possessive instinct unfurls deep within as I stare down at her. My stav aches with the desire to join our bodies as one. I long to claim her and bind her to me in all ways. My nostrils flare as I bask in her delicious scent.

Mine. The word burns through me like fire.

However, she is my mate and will be a princess to our people. I dart a glance at our surroundings. I cannot take her here—not like this. When we mate, I plan to take her several times and for many hours.

"The bond is sealed with our first mating. But I do not wish to take you here."

Her small brow furrows. "Why?"

"Because I want you in my bed and my chambers. I want to take you over and over again, filling you with my essence so that every male within several *arcums* will know that you are mine."

She bites her lower lip again as her cheeks turn a deep shade of red.

Reaching between us, she wraps her hand around my stav. A small crease of worry on her brow gives me pause. Does she dislike the way I feel? "What is wrong?"

"You're so big... and textured," she whispers, her fingers tracing my ridged length. "And I've heard the first time can be a bit painful."

I hate the idea of her experiencing pain from our mating. "Is this normal for your people?"

She nods. "From what I've heard. If we go slow, it's supposed to be easier. But I don't know if making love several times the first night will be... pleasurable," she says a bit hesitantly.

Gently, I skim the tip of my nose along hers as I whisper, "We will go as slow as you need, my linaya. And we will not do anything you do not wish."

She pulls my mouth down to hers and kisses me passionately. My stav aches for release, but I will wait. I will not claim her here. And if our first mating is uncomfortable for her, we will wait as long as she wishes before we mate again.

Gently, she pushes on my shoulders, guiding me onto my back. I willingly comply, for I am hers to do with as she pleases. At first, she leans over me, pressing a series of small kisses to my cheeks, nose, and brow before finally capturing my mouth as she runs her hand across the muscles of my abdomen and chest.

A low growl rumbles inside me as the scent of her need thickens the air again. She enjoys touching me like this.

When she finally pulls away, I am breathless and panting. I reach for her, wanting to kiss her again, but she shakes her head. I open my mouth to speak but snap it shut when she leans down to trail heated kisses along my jaw and neck.

Her hand moves down my body, and the breath explodes

from my lungs when she grips my length and begins to stroke my shaft.

"Your ridges," she whispers, brushing the layers of bumps along my stav.

Worry fills me. "Are they a problem?"

"No. I love the way they feel."

I exhale sharply at her bold words. She brushes her thumb over the tip of my stav, capturing the precum that beads on the end. She lifts one finger to her mouth and I watch, stunned, as she tastes my essence.

She smiles. "You taste like spice and cinnamon."

"Is that a good thing?"

"Yes."

CHAPTER 22

LLYR

She moves down my body, tracing her tongue over the muscles of my chest and abdomen. When she descends, I lift my head, and my jaw drops when she grips my stav and takes me into her mouth. A low groan escapes me as her lips and tongue glide over the tip.

"What are you doing?" I gasp when she licks another bead of precum that rolls down my length.

"What is—"

I cannot form words, much less a coherent thought as she closes her lips over the crown and begins a gentle suction.

"I wanted to taste you like you did me," she whispers.

"You do not have to—" I break off again.

She lowers her head and takes as much of me into her mouth as she can. A strange mixture of pleasure and exquisite torture rush through me with each swipe of her tongue.

"I want to," she whispers, her breath warm against my stav. "You taste so good."

Her words send me over the edge. My head drops, and a low moan passes my lips as she closes her mouth over me again.

She reaches for my hand and guides it to her head. I carefully grasp the long, silken strands between my fingers, careful not to hold her too tightly. It is difficult to maintain my control in her warm, wet mouth.

I have never heard of a Drakarian female doing this, nor a human. If Varus and Raidyn do this with their mates, they never said a word. But the last thing I want is to question her now—not when this feels so good.

My stav is too large for her to take entirely into her mouth; she cannot even wrap her fingers completely around me. But she doesn't need to engulf more than the tip of my crown since her hands glide up and down my length.

I fight to remain still, as I do not want to hurt her. Every muscle in my body is taut as I struggle to hold back my release. I grit my teeth and motion for her to stop.

Instead of stopping, she increases the suction. "You must stop," I rasp. "I will release if you do not, and I—"

She lifts her head just enough to meet my eyes with a heavy-lidded gaze. "Don't hold back, my love," she whispers. "I want you to come." She closes her lips over my crown again and the breath hisses from my lungs.

Her movements quicken as her small hands stroke my length. She swirls her tongue across the tip of my stav and that is my undoing. My release erupts and I watch in wonder as she takes as much of my essence into her mouth as she can. I groan when she gathers the rest with the tips of her fingers and rubs my seed across her bare abdomen and chest, marking her with my scent.

I am still panting heavily as she lies down beside me. Never could I have imagined such pleasure. I twine my arms and wings around her. Dipping my head to the curve of her neck and shoulder, I inhale our combined scent.

"How did you know about the marking?" I ask, replaying in my mind how she rubbed my release across her skin.

Talia smiles. "Lilliana and Skye told me that scent marking is important between mates. It alerts others that a pair has mated."

My stav, still hard after my release, rests against her abdomen. Her eyes widen slightly. "It's true, then," she whispers.

"What?"

"That you don't need time to recover after you climax."

I frown. "Time to… recover?"

A pink bloom spreads across her cheeks. "Lilliana and Skye said that a Drakarian's stav doesn't soften after making love like human men."

This is the first moment I pity human males. How terrible it must be to lose the ability to please one's mate and take her several times in one night while enjoying multiple releases of one's own.

I smile at her. "This is why I want our first mating to happen in my bed in the palace. I will take you for hours on end throughout our first night."

The scent of her need grows more potent with my words and I am once again tempted to claim her fully right now. My gaze drifts toward the sky. A small patch of stars is visible just beyond the lip of the overhang.

"The stars are out," she whispers, having followed my gaze. "Does this mean we can return to the castle?"

I nod, carefully removing my arms and wings from around her. I'm reluctant to leave her embrace, but now that I can navigate, I must fly us home. As I step from beneath the overhang, I immediately spot Silara—the constellation most often used for navigation. I turn to Talia. "We can return home now, my linaya."

She gathers her dress and pulls it over her form with visible excitement. Nudity may be completely acceptable in Drakarian society, but I must admit that I love the knowledge that she bares herself to me and no other. She gathers my robe and shakes off any lingering sand before throwing it over her shoulders as well.

She takes my hand and we walk toward the beach so I can shift into my draka form. I could carry her in this form, but I am stronger and faster in the other, and I am eager to return to the castle. I can only imagine how worried my sister has been all this time, and I am anxious to introduce Talia to my parents.

But first, I must deal with Sorella. I suspect she tried to poison my mate, but I will not know for certain until I can question her.

I turn to Talia, reluctant to remind her of that ordeal, though I must. "When we return, I want you to stay close by my side and then Varus and Raidyn's."

Her brows pinch. "Why Varus and Raidyn?"

"As we discussed, I suspect Sorella is the one who poisoned your food. The only way to convince her to confess is to make her believe that you are leaving me."

"I... don't understand. How will that help?"

"I will be devastated and in need of emotional support." I arch a brow. "Who better to confide in than the female who has expressed a desire to become my mate?"

Her cheeks turn bright red and fire burns in her eyes. "I don't want you anywhere near her. You're mine."

Happiness blooms in my chest at her fierce tone. My mate is already possessive of me, and I find that I enjoy her jealousy immensely. I reach out and cup her cheek. "It is only a ruse, my linaya. I would never touch another. My vow."

She narrows her eyes. "Good. You'd better not."

A wide grin spreads across my face at her sharp command. I gather her in my arms and seal my lips over hers in a passionate kiss. She is strong and fierce. She will be a good mother to our fledglings.

When I finally pull away, she smiles again. "What was that for?"

"Your eyes are full of fire at the mere thought of Sorella approaching me. It pleases me to know you are so possessive of me, my linaya. I did not realize your species had this strong instinct like mine."

"Human men normally don't like a woman who is clingy and possessive."

My opinion of human males drops to new lows. "Then they are fools to reject a dedicated mate."

Before we take off, we discuss a plan to deal with Sorella. The more we plan, the more I must push down my anger. She will pay for trying to harm my linaya.

Setting aside my dark thoughts, I shift into draka form. Talia fidgets nervously and I wonder if I should have opted to carry her in my arms instead. I remember how frightened she was when the Wind Clan attacked and lifted her off the ground. I do not want her to relive her memories of that terrible day.

My nostrils flare as I draw her scent deep into my lungs. I am pleased that she does not smell of fear. I tip my head to the side to regard her. "Are you able to climb onto my back?" I ask, crouching in the sand and extending one leg.

She struggles to pull herself up, so I gently wrap my tail around her waist and lift her the rest of the way, settling her over my shoulders.

"Thanks," she says.

Raidyn and Varus told me they could hear their mate's thoughts in this form, and I am eager to know if it is truth.

The suspense does not last long. As soon as I spread my wings and lift off, my consciousness is flooded with myriad thoughts and images from Talia's mind.

As we fly out over the sea, she fears I might drop her, but that fright soon gives way to wonder as she marvels at the beauty of the ocean, watching in fascination as a school of fish jumps from the waves in formation below.

As soon as the shoreline and my castle come into view, her thoughts become a strange mixture of joy and dread. She is glad to be returning to her friends and our people, but she is also thinking of Sorella, who I suspect may have tried to poison her.

I'm about to reassure her that I will keep her safe, but her mind takes a decidedly erotic turn as she replays images of our time together on the island. My entire body flushes with warmth and my nostrils flare to catch the scent of her arousal. She is excited for me to claim her. I am pleased beyond measure to know that she finds me more appealing than any male she has ever seen.

"As soon as our people are assured we are well and I have dealt with Sorella, I will take you to my chambers and pleasure you thoroughly, my beautiful mate," I tell her. "You will scream my name to the sky as I claim you."

She shivers atop my back—not from the slight chill in the air, I realize, but from arousal.

CHAPTER 23

LLYR

I dip my wing to make a wide arc around the castle. The tide is high and water crashes against the cliff wall below, spraying us with a fine mist as I touch down on the balcony.

Talia swings her leg to dismount, but I shift instantly and wrap my hands around her waist, lowering her body the rest of the way. As soon as her feet touch the ground, I pull her against me and bury my nose in her hair, inhaling deeply of her delicious scent. A growl rumbles my chest as I cup the soft, creamy mound of one breast. I roll the tip between my thumb and forefinger and it immediately stiffens into a hard, beaded tip begging for my attention.

A low moan escapes her as I run my other hand down her body, gathering her dress and slipping my fingers beneath the soft fabric to cup her feminine place. "Tell me you are mine," I breathe in her ear.

"Yours," she breathes. "Only yours."

I am desperate to claim her. Thoughts of tearing the dress

from her form and taking her cloud my mind. But as much as I want her, I must know that she is safe first.

"Let us go greet my Clan so we can enact our plan. Then I will bring you to my rooms and claim you thoroughly, my linaya."

She turns in my arms then stretches on her toes so that her face is even with mine. I drop my forehead to hers and she touches my cheek. "I love you, Llyr."

"I love you too, my beautiful Talia," I whisper in reply. "You have made me the happiest male in existence."

A dazzling smile lights her face as I take her hand and lead her into the hallway. "Come," I tell her. "We will let my people know we have returned."

Although I suspect most of the castle already knows. Several of the guards watched us land on the balcony only a moment ago, and I'm confident they've already reported our safe arrival.

My suspicions are confirmed as soon as we ascend the staircase and Lilliana rushes to greet Talia while my sister Noralla heads straight for me.

"Where were you?" Noralla's eyes meet mine, full of questions. "You disappeared right before the storm."

"We were caught out over the ocean when it hit," I tell her, noting that more people have gathered around us, including Varus, Raidyn, and his mate Skye.

My mother pushes past Noralla and throws her arms around me. "Llyr, I was so worried. Your father and I both." She glances at his approaching form.

As always, my father's face remains stoic, but his eyes betray his happiness and relief to see me. They probably believed me dead or injured all this time.

Talia and I explain to our friends and family what happened, although I note that we both omit the moments of intimacy we shared. That part of our adventure belongs only to us, and I am glad that we wordlessly agree in this regard.

My parents discreetly scent the air as Talia and I speak, but they say nothing. Perhaps they believe we smell so strongly of each other because I flew her here. If they suspect anything else, they do not mention it.

My mother studies her intently as I formally introduce Talia to my parents. I note that she appears rather unimpressed as her gaze rakes over my mate's features. No doubt, taking note of the fact that humans do not possess the natural defenses that Drakarians do. They lack wings, claws, scales and fangs.

I sigh heavily in frustration, for I cannot divulge the truth of everything that happened on the island. Not until I find out if Sorella was behind my poisoning. If I told them I was unconscious at any time during our adventure, it would only lead to questions I cannot answer yet. Not until I discover the truth.

So for now, my parents will not know just how strong my linaya is. I cannot tell them yet of how she saved me and pulled me from the beach to safety after I collapsed; how she cared for me all through the night until I was well again.

My father gives me a questioning look. He knows me well enough to realize that I am holding something back, but he does not ask what it is. That is his way. He will wait for me to tell him. I only wish I could explain everything now so that I might have their blessings on my choice of a mate.

My gaze drifts to Varus, who arches a brow. Raidyn's nostrils flare as he scents the air. He sends me a knowing look and I cannot help the smile that quirks my mouth as I return a subtle nod.

I cannot wait to ask them about their mates, for I want to understand human females to make sure Talia is well and thoroughly pleasured when I claim her.

"Where's Anna?" Talia asks.

"She left with Prince Kaj," Lilliana answers.

Varus and Raidyn exchange a glance, moving to my side. Varus speaks first. "We have not heard from them. They disappeared when you and Talia did. A few of the humans claimed they saw Kaj and Anna kissing on the balcony shortly before he flew her away."

My brow furrows. "Do you believe they are mated then, even though he told us she rejected him?"

Raidyn nods. "Kaj is an honorable male. He would not have stolen her away against her will."

Varus arches a teasing brow at him. "Unlike *someone* I know."

Raidyn huffs. "I did not steal my mate. I *saved* her."

Skye wraps her arm around his waist. "Everyone knows you saved me, my love."

Raidyn leans down to press a kiss to her temple before straightening and narrowing his eyes at Varus.

Varus laughs, though his expression quickly sobers. "If we do not hear from them soon, we should search for them."

He looks to his mate and she nods. "I'm just worried something may have happened," she says.

I open my mouth to protest that Kaj would never harm a female, but Lilliana puts her hand up in a bid to speak. "I'm not concerned that Kaj would harm Anna, but worried that something may have happened to them both."

"Ah." I understand. "Kaj is strong. I cannot imagine he could come to any harm."

"Neither can I," Varus adds. "But we are concerned, none-theless."

"I will help you search, if it comes to that," I promise.

"Thank you, my friend." He glances at Talia, who is now talking to Skye. Lilliana moves to join them. He continues. "It seems you have convinced her to accept you."

I smile for a moment before my expression sobers. "I must speak with you both. Privately." Their eyes flash with concern, but I place a hand on Varus's shoulder. "All will make sense shortly."

He nods.

I'm certain Sorella will be able to detect Talia's scent upon me as well, but I hope that will not matter. Talia will leave as we discussed, and Sorella will believe I have been rejected.

As if my very thoughts have summoned her, Sorella walks up the stairs. Her sharp gaze rakes over Talia's form, not bothering to hide her disgust. I'm convinced she tried to poison my mate. No one else has motive.

CHAPTER 24

LLYR

I t was torture sleeping without Talia in my arms last night after our return. This morning, I feel sick watching Varus carry both his mate and mine upon his back to return to the Fire Clan territory. I stand on the balcony, watching them climb into the clouds and disappear. I can easily feign heartbreak over Talia's departure, for this is exactly how I felt when I had to leave her in the Fire lands many days ago.

Movement to my right side draws my attention, and I turn to find Sorella approaching me with pity written on her face. "The human refused you, did she not?"

I lower my gaze to my hands and nod with false reluctance. "She does not want me."

"Then she is a fool," Sorella states firmly.

With a heavy sigh, I turn my gaze out to sea. "I thought she would want me after I proved my ability to provide for her needs. She was ill when we first landed on the island. I took care of her for two days."

Sorella moves closer. "Her species *is* very fragile. Perhaps it is for the best that you did not mate such a pitiful creature. Your fledglings would be weak and unable to hold the throne."

Anger flares inside me, but I force it down. Slowly, I lift my eyes to hers. "If I did not know any better, I would believe she had been poisoned."

She stills.

"You wouldn't know anything about that, would you?"

"Llyr, I—"

"Think very carefully before you answer, Sorella," I warn. "Even now, your rooms are being searched, and the servant who served us dinner is being questioned."

She gapes at me. "I—I only meant to protect you, Llyr. Those creatures should not be mating with our people. Their weakness would tarnish your bloodline."

"Then you admit it?" I arch a brow.

She trembles, pleading, "I did it for you. You are the prince of the Water Clan. You deserve better than that pitiful female."

"That is not for *you* to decide," I grind out.

Frantic eyes meet mine. "What will you do?"

"You are hereby banished from Water Clan territory."

"You cannot do this!"

"I am the prince. It is already done. You have one day to gather your things while we inform your family of your disgrace." I turn to the doorway as Arnav, my most trusted guard, steps across the threshold. "Take her away."

"Come with me," he commands Sorella sternly, his deep blue eyes thunderous as his purple scales darken with anger.

"And what if I refuse?"

"We will drag you from the palace if we must," he states firmly. "But my prince has ordered your removal, and I vow that it will be done."

To my surprise, Sorella follows Arnav quietly.

I am eager to return to my mate, who should even now be circling back to the castle. Varus was instructed to turn around as soon as he was out of sight. Noralla agreed to take Talia to my rooms and instruct her to wait until after I dealt with Sorella.

As I turn to head for my rooms, Noralla walks onto the balcony, beaming. "Talia is in your suite."

I can hardly wait to pull her into my arms, but I know I must speak with my parents first. I must inform them that Talia has agreed to be mine. They knew I loved her when I returned from the Fire Clan, but they too believed that she had rejected me.

Only my sister, Varus, Raidyn, and their mates knew of our plan. The deception was necessary since my parents are terrible at keeping secrets and might have given us away.

As it was, my mother's tears at my anguish were genuine and more than convincing to Sorella. However, I feel guilty and must apologize to my parents at once.

When I walk to their chambers my mother rushes to me, embracing me warmly. "Oh, my son. I am so sorry that terrible female rejected you."

My father clears his throat beside her. "If she rejected you, she was unworthy of your love to begin with."

A smile tugs at my lips at their fierce love and devotion for me. I pull back and give my mother a hesitant look. I hate that I had to lie to them. "It was all a lie," I explain.

Mother blinks several times. "What do you mean?"

"Talia loves me. She has agreed to be mine."

Father frowns. "I do not understand. I thought she left because she did not want you."

Noralla steps forward, she darts a glance at me and then turns her attention back to our parents. "We wanted to tell you, but you are both terrible liars. Sorella would have picked up on it right away."

"What does Sorella have to do with this?" Mother asks.

As I explain everything that happened, my mother's scales pale slightly as she listens to how I was poisoned. When I explain how brave and strong Talia is, and how she took care of me while I was unconscious, my parents give me a stunned look.

Father places a hand on my shoulder. "She is strong, your linaya."

"Yes," Mother agrees. "It seems I was wrong about the humans. Take me to her. I would like to welcome her formally into our family."

A beaming smile lights my face, and I turn back to Noralla.

"Thank you so much for your help, my dear sister."

"I am simply glad you are happy, Llyr." Her gaze drops to my chest, searching for the fate mark. She arches a brow. "I thought she would not accept you without the mark. What changed her mind?"

"She is brave, my mate," I tell her, smiling to myself at the memory. "Willing to risk everything to be with the male she loves."

Father takes Mother's hands in his and gently presses a kiss to her knuckles as he stares at her lovingly. "Your mother took a chance on me as well. She agreed to bond with me before the fate mark appeared." He turns to me. "You have chosen well, my son. I am happy for you, and—"

Arnav rushes onto the balcony, his eyes wide. "Sorella has escaped!"

Alarm bursts through me. "How?"

I lift my gaze to the sky, hoping to catch her flying away. When I do not spot her, long tendrils of fear unfurl in my chest and wrap around my spine.

"Who is guarding my chambers?" I ask, my thoughts turning immediately to Talia's safety.

"Onaril and Vanir," he replies.

Even though my room is guarded, a knot of worry twists in my stomach. Sorella has been banished, yet only a handful of people know of her crime and punishment. She could even now be walking the castle halls unchallenged, placing Talia in danger.

I rush past Arnav and shout over my shoulder, "Quickly! Follow me!"

CHAPTER 25

TALIA

I anxiously pace back and forth in Llyr's room. I can hardly wait to see him. It was difficult having to act distant, even for less than a day. But Noralla told me that his plan worked—Sorella is banished and we are finally free to begin our life together.

Varus and Lilly promised to visit as often as possible, and Raidyn and Skye said the same. I lament settling down so far from my friends, but I love Llyr. I can't imagine my life without him anymore.

On the other hand, Milo was not thrilled when he found out about our plan. He was so happy when he thought I was rejecting Llyr, so when he discovered that was all a lie, he was upset. I understand; he's my brother, and he worries about me. He doesn't want me to get hurt.

I told him he could stay in the castle with Llyr and me, but he's still undecided. I hope he'll choose to live with us. After all, he'd be the only other human in the Water Clan territory.

My gaze drifts to the king-size bed floating in the center of the room. I marvel at the ocean scenes that decorate the light gray wooden headboard and the intricate shapes carved into the bedposts. The fluffy white comforter looks so inviting. Heat fills my entire body as I imagine Llyr wrapping me up in his arms beneath the blankets.

This palace is beautiful, and I can hardly believe this will be my new home.

I look toward the balcony. The sheer white panels covering the doors billow with the cool ocean breeze that drifts in. The sound of water crashing against the shoreline relaxes me. In all my wildest dreams about the world we'd one day settle on, I never imagined it could be this amazing.

My thoughts turn to his family, and I swallow hard against the knot of worry in my stomach. We need to speak with his parents, though I don't know how they'll feel about their son mating a human. His mother did not seem all that thrilled when she saw me earlier—before she thought I'd rejected her son.

In fact, she was probably happy when she thought I was leaving him for good.

Llyr assured me they will accept me, but I remember Lilly told me that Varus's parents opposed their bonding at first, just as Raidyn's father didn't approve of Skye. Surely now that Llyr's parents have seen how happy Prince Varus and King Raidyn are with their mates, they will give us their blessing.

I hope.

The doors *whoosh* open and I spin toward the doorway, smiling as I wait for Llyr to step inside. My expression falls when Sorella enters.

Her sharp gaze scans me from head to toe with revulsion. "Why are you here?"

"What are *you* doing here?" I counter. "You're supposed to be exiled."

She narrows her yellow eyes. "And you're supposed to be dead."

"Leave." I grit my teeth. "Now."

A low, menacing growl vibrates her chest as she levels an icy glare at me. Her dark claws lengthen into sharpened points as she bares her teeth in a feral snarl. "I will make sure to finish the job this time."

She starts toward me and I stumble back, bumping my hip against a bedside table. Her gaze holds mine as she advances like a predator stalking its prey. I dart a glance around the room for something to use as a weapon but find nothing.

She lunges and I hastily spin away. She crashes into the table, shattering the glass surface and scattering the broken pieces across the room.

Lightning fast, I grab one of the larger shards. The sharp edges score my palm, but I brandish my weapon firmly. I can defend myself—that's all that matters.

I refuse to die today.

CHAPTER 26

LLYR

My hearts stop at the sound of breaking glass echoing from inside my room. I rush through the door with Arnav close behind me. We both freeze when we spot Talia holding a jagged shard of glass in one hand as she faces down Sorella.

Rage boils through my veins as I notice crimson blood dripping to the floor from Talia's palm. "How dare you attack my mate?" I snarl at Sorella. "If you touch her, I will kill you."

"You are too late," she sneers, her eyes locked on my linaya. "All you can do is watch her die."

"Llyr!" Talia calls out.

Sorella whips her head back toward Talia. The world slows as she rushes toward my mate. My feet cannot carry me fast enough, and I know I won't reach them in time.

Sorella barrels into my linaya, slamming her back against the wall. A scream pierces the room and my hearts stutter when they both go still and slide to the floor. I grip Sorella's forearms firmly and yank her off my mate, stunned when I find the broken shard of glass embedded deep in the Drakarian female's throat.

Sorella's eyes are wide with shock. Black blood pours from the wound and pools on the floor beneath her. I watch the light fade from her gaze.

I turn my attention to my linaya. "Talia? Are you all right?" I reach for the injured palm she cradles in her other hand. "Let me see."

Shakily, she extends her hand to me. I rip a strip of cloth from her dress and wrap it tightly around the wound as I call over my shoulder, "Get the Healer! Now!"

"It's just my hand." Her voice quavers. "I—"

I pull her into my arms, running my fingers through her long, silken hair. I press a series of kisses to her cheeks, brow, and nose before finally reaching her mouth. "Thank the gods you are all right, my linaya."

I could have lost her in an instant. I have failed as a protector. She will not want me now.

Healer Rijan rushes in. He stares down at Sorella's dead body, stunned. "What happened?" he breathes out. "How did—"

"She attacked my mate," I state firmly, snapping him out of the trance-like state of shock he seems to be in. "Sorella tried to kill Talia."

He blinks as if coming back to himself and then drops to his knees before her. "Allow me to treat your wound."

Talia holds out her hand and he peels back the fabric, his healing fire mending her injury. Her shoulders sag against me as the pain slowly ebbs away under his ministrations.

When he is finished, he uses another bandage to wrap her hand. "The pain is gone, yes?"

She nods.

"The skin should be fully healed by the morning. If you need anything else, do not hesitate to call for me."

"Thank you." She manages a faint smile.

The guards remove Sorella's body from the room and then begin cleaning the space to erase any evidence of what happened here.

As soon as Healer Rijan leaves, I wrap Talia protectively in my arms and wings. This is probably the last time she will allow me to touch her. I have failed in every possible way to protect her; she was forced to save herself. A Drakarian female would never take such an unworthy male. Desperately, I nuzzle her hair and breathe in her scent, trying to memorize every part of her before she leaves me forever.

I'm vaguely aware of my parents entering, and only because Arnav's explanation of the chaos littering the room reaches my ears.

My mother approaches and gently touches Talia's forearm. "Are you all right?"

Talia's fragile form is still trembling in my arms. She is no doubt in shock over what just happened. Nevertheless, she lifts her blue eyes to my mother's and mumbles, "I'm just a bit shaken, that's all. I'm sure I'll be fine in a moment."

My hearts clench. My strong, brave female. How could anyone doubt the strength of her people? She is perfect, and I will lose her because I broke my vow that she would be safe with me.

Mother tips her head to the side to regard her. "You are very brave and also very strong. Llyr told us about how you saved him."

"Yes," my father agrees behind her. "We have heard much about you. How can we ever repay you for saving our son?"

She shakes her head softly. "You do not owe me anything. Your son and I saved each other. I love him."

Mother's eyes light up. "I am glad to hear this. We would like to welcome you to our family if you will still have my son as your mate." She darts a glance at my father and smiles.

"But for now, we will leave you two alone so that you may decide upon your future."

"Thank you," Talia smiles up at them.

Talia's statement that she loves me gives me hope. I pray that she will still accept me as her mate, despite my failure. But even if she no longer desires me, I still wish to care for her.

My parents leave the room. I cast a quick glance around the space, satisfied that it has been thoroughly cleaned. With Talia cradled in my arms, I make my way to the cleansing room.

She turns to me, frowning. "What are you doing?"

"I'm going to care for you, Talia. Will you allow me to?"

She nods.

Satisfied, I walk us toward the warm, sunken pool in the center of the floor.

CHAPTER 27

TALIA

Llyr carefully removes my dress and discards it on the floor of the cleansing room. The water is warm on my skin as he carries me into the pool. It seems both the Fire and Water Clans build their bathrooms from the same design. The space is nothing short of palatial. Fine silver finishes and beautifully painted tile lend an elegance to the room. The huge pool in the center of the floor could easily fit four people and has a sunken bench like the one I had in the Fire castle.

Gently, Llyr cleanses me with a soft towel, washing the blood off my skin. He moves his hands in small circular motions, slowly unknotting all the tension in my muscles. He lifts me into his lap and I close my eyes, leaning against his chest and allowing myself to practically melt in his arms.

"Thank you," I whisper, turning my head to face him.

He simply nods. It's only now that I notice the sadness shining in his eyes as he silently bathes me. I reach up to touch his face, drawing his attention back to me. "What's wrong?"

"I have failed you," he mutters, so low I almost miss it. "Forgive me."

I don't understand what he's talking about. "Why are you saying that? You didn't fail me."

His eyes snap up to meet mine, full of guilt. "You almost died because I failed to protect you."

"It's not your fault that Sorella attacked me, Llyr. Why would you think I would blame you?"

His brow furrows deeply. "A Drakarian female would. She would consider me unworthy because she was attacked and placed in danger after I vowed to protect her."

My mouth drifts open. No wonder he is so upset—he thinks I'm going to leave him. I turn in his arms so that my thighs straddle his hips. Twining my arms around his neck, I meet his gaze evenly. "I love you, Llyr." Gently, I press a soft kiss to his mouth. "I'm not going to reject you and I will never leave you, my love."

"You would still be mine?" I note the hint of caution in his voice as if he's afraid what I'm saying is too good to be true.

I brush my mouth over his and smile against his lips. "Yes. Make love to me. Bind me to you as your mate."

He wraps his wings around me, pulling me close. His tongue finds mine, deepening our kiss. A low moan escapes me as the ridges of his tongue brush my lips, reminding me of the delicious ridges of his *stav*.

His breath escapes him in a sharp hiss as I reach between us and trace my fingers over his length. "Need you," he rasps. "Now."

"Take me to bed," I whisper. "I want you."

He carries me from the pool and presses a small glowing panel on the wall. A mechanical wand extends from the ceiling and passes over us, creating small vibrations along my skin. A small huff of air escapes me when I realize my entire body and my hair are completely dry.

I'm about to ask Llyr to show me how to activate this dryer in the future, but when my eyes meet his, my breath hitches in my throat. His pupils are blown wide so that only a thin rim of silver is visible around the edges. He stalks to our bed and pulls back the cover, laying me beneath the blankets.

His gaze is fiery and possessive. My heart hammers in my chest as he crawls over my body. He snakes his tail around my left thigh, gently parting my legs as he settles between them.

The crown of his *stav* bumps the entrance to my core, and I gasp. He reaches between us and runs his fingers through my already slick folds. "You are ready for me, my mate?" His voice is a low rumble as his eyes remain locked on mine.

I reach up and trace my fingers across the sharp ridge of his brow before cupping his cheek. "Always, my love."

CHAPTER 28

LLYR

My entire body fills with warmth at her words. I can hardly believe this beautiful female is mine. That she chooses me when she could have anyone is humbling beyond words.

Talia inhales sharply, reaching up to touch my chest. I look down. The fate mark pattern glows brightly across the scales between my hearts. A radiant smile lights my face. It shines for her, just as I always knew it would.

I place my hand over hers on my chest. "I knew," I whisper. "From the first moment I saw you, my linaya."

"You were right." She looks up at me, her eyes full of tears. "We're meant to be together."

"You are mine," I press my lips to hers in a branding kiss. "And now I will claim you, my beautiful mate. I will bind you to me so that all will know you are mine and I am yours."

I had planned, for our initial mating, to pleasure her with my mouth first, but the sight of her body beneath me is too tempting to ignore. The crown of my stav is notched at the

175

entrance to her core, and she gasps. My nostrils flare as the scent of her arousal grows more potent and she wraps her legs around my hips.

Her folds are already slick with her arousal. I desire more than anything to sink my stav deep into her channel and fill her with my essence.

"The scent of your need calls to me, my mate," I growl. "Forgive me, but I can wait no longer."

I stare deep into her eyes as I slowly enter her, watching for any sign of discomfort. She's so tight I grit my teeth as I force myself to move slowly, worried that I might harm her. Her lips part on a soft moan as I sheathe myself deep inside her, gently rocking my hips back and forth as I advance.

Her warm, wet heat envelopes me and my mind goes blank as overwhelming pleasure floods my veins. My stav twitches as soon as I am fully seated inside her, releasing a burst of precum into her channel.

Her head tips back and she moans again at the sensation. "So warm," she breathes. "That feels so good. What was that?"

She arches her hips against mine, and I grit my teeth as I struggle to hold back my release. I long more than anything to fill her completely, but I want to bring her pleasure first. "It is some of my essence, softening your womb to accept my seed."

Her nails dig into my back as I begin a slow and steady rhythm, stroking deep into her channel. Soft moans escape her with each thrust. She pants my name, asking for more. I want to be gentle, but she tightens her legs around me and my control begins to slip.

"You're so tight," I rasp. "I don't want to hurt you."

She grips the back of my neck, pulling my lips down to hers. "I'm not going to break, Llyr. You don't have to hold back. I want you, my love. All of you."

The last of my control crumbles at her words. I wrap my

tail around her thigh and brace my arm under her leg, opening her even more to accept me. A low groan escapes my throat as I sink even deeper into her channel. She holds me tightly as I thrust into her, each stroke becoming more forceful and desperate. It is the most exquisite torture to hold back my release.

"Llyr, I'm so close," she whispers. "Please."

I clench my jaw, increasing my pace. The delicious friction of my stav moving deep inside her is almost overwhelming and I worry I might spill inside her before she comes. Although I can release many times without tiring, I want her to find her release before me. Primal possessiveness fills me. I want her body primed and ready to accept my seed, to take every last drop of my essence.

The small muscles of her channel begin to quiver and flex around my length. I wrap my hand around her hip, holding her in place as I thrust long and deep.

My body hums in awareness of hers and I can think of nothing outside of this moment with my mate as I stare deep into her eyes. She is mine, and I want only to give her pleasure.

My name escapes her lips in a breathless moan as she runs her hands down the length of my back, tracing the muscles along my spine as I pump into her. Her entire body goes taut a moment and then she cries out my name as she falls over the edge and into her climax.

Unable to hold back any longer, my stav begins to pulse deep in her core. "Mine," I roar as my release erupts from my body, filling her with my seed.

The beautiful moment feels as though it goes on forever as my essence floods her open womb. She is mine, and I already want to take her again. My stav is still hard and buried deep inside her as I lean down and press my lips to hers.

"That was more than I ever imagined it could be," she whispers. "I love you, Llyr."

She stares up at me with a half-lidded gaze. Tenderly, I skim the tip of my nose along hers then drop my head to the curve of her neck, inhaling deeply of our combined scent.

"Are you in any pain, my linaya?" I ask because I will not take her again if she is.

She brushes her fingers across my lips as her eyes meet mine, full of love. "No, my love. I'm fine."

Desire fills me. I begin to move my hips against hers again, and she gasps. "You want me again so soon?"

I brush the damp hair from her face to meet her rich, blue eyes. "My mating heat has begun. I plan to take you several times this evening, my linaya."

Her small brow furrows softly. "Your… mating heat?"

I nod and press my lips to hers once more. "A male's heat is only triggered when his mate is at her fertile peak."

She blinks. "You're all right if we get pregnant so soon?"

I begin long, languid strokes deep inside her. The mere thought of my seed taking root in her womb stirs my desire even more. "I want everything with you, my beautiful mate."

A stunning smile curves her lips. "I want everything with you too, my love."

EPILOGUE

TALIA

As I stand on the balcony and watch the sun slowly rise from the deep, blue ocean below, I smile. I've never been happier. Each day I spend with Llyr is better than the one before. His parents are wonderful and fully accept me as their daughter. Noralla is as close as a sister to me. I feel so blessed; I can hardly believe this is my life. I never knew such joy existed.

Warm arms wrap around me from behind and pull me back against a solid, warm chest. I sigh, snuggling into my mate as he dips his head and presses a soft kiss to my neck. He inhales deeply as a low growl vibrates in his chest. "Your scent is intoxicating, my linaya."

Llyr insists that I'm already carrying our child, but I think it's too soon to tell. We'll go to the Healer this afternoon and find out if he's right.

He slides one hand down my body, resting his open palm over my lower abdomen. "Your people and our fledglings are the future of my race," he murmurs in my ear. "Before you arrived, we were four separate Clans, constantly on the brink of war. Because of you, we have established peace."

I turn in his arms to face him. "Have you heard any news from the search parties? Has more of my crew been found?"

He shakes his head. "Not yet. But do not give up hope, my linaya. The universe is vast. We will not give up so easily. My vow."

I was surprised by how many ships Drakaria has committed to finding more survivors on the planet and across the entire system. They're good people, and we are lucky to have landed on their world.

My thoughts turn to my parents. I choose to hold on to the hope that I'll see them again someday. Milo thinks I'm foolish, but I don't care.

Speaking of Milo...

I meet Llyr's eyes evenly. "I have some news you may not like, my love."

He stills, worry flashing in his gaze. "What is wrong?"

"My brother wants to move in with us."

Llyr's shoulders relax. "Your brother is welcome to live in the castle. But what changed his mind? I thought he did not like me."

I chuckle. "It's not that he dislikes you, Llyr. He's just being overprotective of his sister."

Llyr smiles and pulls me close to his chest. "I understand. I feel the same way about Noralla." He arches a brow. "Your brother will like the castle. I believe that, given enough time, we will become great friends."

"I don't think that will be as easy as you anticipate," I tease.

"I hope that his protective nature extends to our fledglings. He will be a good uncle, I believe."

I roll my eyes, shaking my head in mock frustration. "You're absolutely sure we're having twins, aren't you?"

"You will see that I am right." He places his palm on his chest, directly over the fate mark. "I feel it here." He lifts his hands and crooks two fingers to make air quotations. "Trust me, my linaya."

I laugh. Even after I explained the proper use of air quotations to him, he keeps using them wrong. However, I find his mistake endearing and he knows it. So the quotes have become our own private joke.

"Well, let's see what the Healer has to say, shall we?" I tease, using air quotes as well.

He laughs again, but then his expression changes. Hunger enters his gaze. His hands slide down my body to cup my backside, dragging me closer.

"I do not need the Healer to tell me the truth I know in my hearts. Your scent calls to me, Talia." He growls, low and aroused. "I need you."

I open my mouth to speak, but he seals his lips over mine and carries me into the bedroom. Gently, he lays me on the bed and moves over me. He watches me, his eyes full of love and devotion.

"You are perfect, Talia. The gods granted me more than I could ever have asked for, when they sent you to me."

I feel the same way. I reach up to place my palm over the glowing fate mark on his chest, wondering how I could have ever doubted his love before the pattern appeared. "I love you so much, Llyr."

He braces his elbows on either side of my body and then crooks the first two fingers of each hand, making air quotations as he smiles down at me. "I love you too, my beautiful linaya."

181

ABOUT ARIA WINTER

Thank you so much for reading this. I hope you enjoyed this story. If you enjoyed this book, please leave a review on Amazon and/or Goodreads. I would really appreciate it. Reviews are the lifeblood of Indie Authors.

Other works by Aria Winter:

Elemental Dragon Warriors Series
   Claimed by the Fire Dragon Prince
   Stolen by the Wind Dragon Prince
   Rescued by the Water Dragon Prince
   Healed by the Earth Dragon Prince

Want more Dragon Shifter Romance? Try my Fairy Tale Series
   Once Upon A Fairy Tale Romance Series
   Taken by the Dragon: A Beauty and the Beast Retelling
   Captivated by the Fae: A Cinderella Retelling
   Rescued By The Merman: A Little Mermaid Retelling
   Bound to the Elf Prince: A Snow White Retelling

Cosmic Guardian Series
   Charmed by the Fox's Heart
   Seduced by the Peacock's Beauty
   Protected by the Spider's Web
   Ensnared by the Serpent's Gaze
   Forged by the Dragon's Flame

Once Upon a Shifter Series
Ella and her Shifters

For information about upcoming releases Like me on Facebook (http://www.facebook.com/ariawinterauthor)
or sign up for upcoming release alerts at my website:

Ariawinter.com

ABOUT JADE WALTZ

Jade Waltz lives in Illinois with her husband, two sons, and her three crazy cats. She loves knitting, playing video games, and watching Esports. Jade's passions include the arts, green tea and mints — all while writing and teaching marching band drill in the fall.

Jade has always been an avid reader of the fantasy, paranormal and sci-fi genres and wanted to create worlds she always wanted to read.

She writes character driven romances within detailed universes, where happily-ever-afters happen for those who dare love the abnormal and the unknown. Their love may not be easy—but it is well worth it in the end.

Thank you for taking the time to read my book!
Please leave a review!
Reviews are important for indie self-publishing authors and they help us grow.

Website: www.jadewaltz.com
Facebook Author Page: Jade Waltz
Facebook Group: Jade Waltz Literary Alcove
Twitter: @authorjadewaltz
Instagram: @authorjadewaltz
Email: authorjadewaltz@gmail.com
Amazon Profile: Jade Waltz

Bookbub: Jade Waltz

Project Universe Timeline:

Project: Adapt #1 – Found
Project Adapt #2 - Achieve
Project: Adapt #3 – Develop
Project: Adapt #4 - Failure

Project: F5 #1 – Bird of Prey
Project: F5 #2 – Scaled Heart

Project: Adapt #4 – Failure

Elemental Dragon Warriors:

Claimed by the Fire Dragon Prince
Stolen by the Wind Dragon Prince
Rescued by the Water Dragon Prince
Healed by the Earth Dragon Prince

Cosmic Guardian Series

Charmed by the Fox's Heart
Seduced by the Peacock's Beauty
Protected by the Spider's Web
Ensnared by the Serpent's Gaze
Forged by the Dragon's Flame

Printed in Great Britain
by Amazon

56897810R00116